the PHANTOM DETECTIVE

AIRSHIP 27 PRODUCTIONS

The Phantom Detective Volume One

Published by Airship 27 Productions
www.airship27.com
www.airship27hangar.com

Editor: Ron Fortier
Associate Editor: Gordon Dymowski
Marketing and Promotions Manager: Michael Vance
Production and design by Rob Davis

ISBN-10: 0-9977868-9-2
ISBN-13: 978-0-9977868-9-7

Printed in the United States of America

10 9 8 7 6 5 4 3 2 1

Volume One

Table of Contents

THE PHANTOM MENACE...5
By Gary Lovisi
When the Mayor orders the police to capture the Phantom Detective, Richard Curtis Van Loan goes from being a masked vigilante to a wanted outlaw.

CIRCLE OF DESPAIR...32
By Gene Moyers
The murders of several prominent men leads the Phantom Detective to a small, Connecticut College and a group of once idealistic young men.

CAMPAIGN OF DESTRUCTION.......................................72
By Whit Howland
G-Man Dan Fowler works with the Phantom Detective to save the city from a crooked politician threatening to destroy New York City to achieve his goals.

HARBOR LIGHTS..114
By Robert Ricci
When the Clarion publisher, Frank Haven's daughter, Muriel, disappears while on a reporting jaunt to Boston, it's up to the Phantom Detective to wing his way to Beantown and rescue her.

THE DEVIL'S MINIONS...159
By Gary Lovisi
A mysterious criminal called the Devil is spreading fear throughout the city and only the Phantom Detective can stop him.

The Phantom Menace
by Gary Lovisi

"I tell you, Dick, he's a menace to our city. This Phantom, Phantom Detective, or whatever you want to call him, is no better than our criminal 'friend' Big Nose," Mayor Rogers stated to the well-dressed, handsome young man seated to his right at the table of notables that evening at New York's prestigious Stork Club. The event was to celebrate the Mayor's re-election, so Rogers and his wife had invited some of the cities' most powerful and influential movers and shakers to a special dinner. On the top of that list, of course, was the wealthy playboy, Richard Curtis Van Loan.

"You make the Phantom sound as bad as Big Nose Marino, Mayor," Frank Havens quickly stepped in to defend the masked crime fighter, "by mentioning a man rumored by some to be a crime kingpin; surely you can not compare him to the masked Phantom?"

The Mayor just shook his head, "He may be worse."

Now playboy Van Loan answered the Mayor, "Well, I have it on good authority this masked man absolutely hates crime -- though no one knows who he is."

Then Van Loan glanced knowingly across the table towards his friend, Frank Havens. Newspaper magnet and *Clarion* publisher Frank Havens was the only person who knew the true identity of the masked crime fighter known as The Phantom.

"Sorry, Van, but I am not convinced," Mayor Rogers added tersely.

Van Loan continued, "Mr. Mayor, all I know is what I hear, and what I read in the papers like *The Clarion*, and that is, that this Phantom does good work catching criminals the police can not. You can not compare him to a man like Marino at all."

Police Chief Hayes took a thoughtful sip of his martini, then looked at the young man seated across from him, "That may very well be true, Mr. Van Loan, but I have a theory that this Phantom may have something more sinister at heart. This Phantom may just be smarter than the usual criminal we have to deal with, passing himself off as a heroic crime fighter. I ask you, why does he wear a mask? What is he trying to hide?"

There was silence at the table for a long moment. The diners knew this could be a touchy subject among some of those seated there, such as publisher Frank Havens whose papers heralded the many accomplishments of The Phantom. The entire city was recently focused on the masked avenger wondering if he was truly against crime and for the police, as Haven's *Clarion* touted; or just another criminal himself. Some believed he might be some mastermind seeking dominance over the New York criminal underworld. They argued that, surely, that would prove him to be a monumental danger if true. A lot more dangerous than someone like Albert "Big Nose" Marino, who was rumored to be the man behind crime in the city, but as yet, had never been touched by the law.

Before Van Loan could answer Chief Hayes, Frank Havens jumped into the conversation once again, "Look, Chief, we all know the Phantom has proved to be an ace crime fighter. Why, he's even captured criminals your department was unable to apprehend. Perhaps there is some jealously there, eh?"

The Police Chief's face grew beet red with embarrassment, then he swallowed hard, said, "I admit he's been helpful in the past, but what is his purpose? And again, I ask, why the mask?"

"Perhaps, this Phantom merely seeks to do good without reaping any publicity for his noble acts," said the young and lovely Muriel Havens, daughter of *Clarion* publisher Frank Havens.

Richard Curtis Van Loan smiled at the lovely young woman seated next to her father. He was entranced by her fire-red hair, red inviting lips, the way her lovely shoulders shone in the low-cut evening gown she wore so perfectly. He was fascinated by Muriel, his best friend's daughter, secretly desirous of her for his wife -- yet a wife he could not have and a life he could not live. For Van Loan had a secret that could mean his doom, and the doom of anyone he loved. His secret was that *he* was in fact the fabled Phantom Detective and that made it impossible for him to ever conceive of anything approaching a normal life. Not for him was a life with the woman he loved, marriage, a home, and children. These were the things he wanted most in life, yet it was just too dangerous for those closest to him, so he must forego them and remain alone.

Van Loan sighed then smiled, "Miss Havens may be correct. I imagine this masked man, whoever he may be, just wants to do his part to stop crime in his own way. Surely there can be nothing wrong with that?"

"Vigilantism, Mr. Van Loan, is what is wrong with it," now spoke up Evan Jones for the first time as he had been following the conversation with alarm. He was a wealthy banker whose business interests ran the gamut throughout the city. "I think Mayor Rogers and Police Chief Hayes can agree, that we must not allow some masked vigilante to run around New York making his own laws and enforcing them in his own manner. I mean, gentlemen and ladies this is, after all, 1936, not the Wild West! Even Prohibition has seen its end, thankfully by the way, and so should this masked vigilante."

"I disagree," Frank Havens answered sternly. "The Phantom is a force for good in our city. He has captured, or caused to have captured by your police, Chief Hayes, dozens of the cities most notorious villains. We should be thankful that such a man exists and is willing to put his life on the line, not for pay or publicity, for he receives none, but to protect the people of our fair city. I for one am thankful for all his good deeds."

"Well said, Frank," Simon Tallridge blurted between sips of wine. He was a rich industrialist whose businesses spawned wealth and power in abundance throughout the city. "The man deserves all our thanks, whoever he might be."

Havens looked at Van Loan and allowed a grim smile that denoted the Phantom had some allies among this powerful group. Havens was the only person at that table, the only person in the world, who knew that Richard Curtis Van Loan was the Phantom Detective and the two had a relationship that went back since Van had come home from The Great War.

"Well," Mayor Rogers began seriously, "it's an interesting argument, but it takes us nowhere, I'm afraid. The decision has been made. I concur with Chief Hayes, and that is, that this man, this Phantom, could very well be a menace and a real danger. Until we know otherwise, I am ordering Chief Hayes to use all the powers of his department to track down and capture this masked man. Then we shall rip the mask from his face and discover who he truly is. I will not allow a masked avenger to run around my city in disguise for reasons we do not know. The man could be nothing more than some super criminal seeking to concentrate his power over underworld leaders by turning in his rivals to the police. Now, I admit, on the face if it, that has been good for the city and the police to have these men arrested, but what is to come, gentleman, ladies, what is to come of it all?"

Frank Havens just shook his head in dismay, "I think this is a bad move, Mr. Mayor. The Phantom has proven his adherence to law and order over and over again. He is beloved by the police and our citizens. The man is on *our* side! Not only is your plan unfair, it may cause him to put an end to his crime fighting activities, and that would be a disaster for this city."

"If he is innocent, he has nothing to fear," Chief Hayes added smugly, finishing his martini in one gulp. "We just want to discover his true identity."

"But he doesn't want you to know who he is," Van Loan spoke up, a bit too forcefully.

"Well, that's just the way it has to be, Van," Mayor Rogers told the young playboy with a winning smile.

"Then I think that will stop his activities, and I fear people may die because of it," Van Loan warned, then curtly shut himself off, fearing he had spoken too much, much too forcefully. Van was supposed to be the epitome of the futile and pampered playboy, never allowing his emotions to rise up to advocate forcefully for his alter ego The Phantom. After all, what did rich playboy Richard Curtis Van Loan care about such things?

"I have to agree with Van," Frank Havens added, "however, you can not stop a man like The Phantom."

"That may be fine for you, Frank," banker Evan Jones added, lighting a cigar, "he gives your papers scoops on crime and criminal captures, like those robbers who took down my bank last month, or the Landenburg Kidnapping Case. He's good for your newspaper business, my friend. His actions make headlines, but I have to admit I am grateful he caught the gang that robbed my First National, back in May. Though I am sure that Chief Hayes' men would have caught the gang, eventually."

Chief Hayes looked up at that comment. He wasn't quite sure if the remark had been a subtle slight or a mild accolade, so he kept mum.

The discussion turned to other topics as the waiters brought over the entrees. Succulent roast duck, grilled pheasant, fillet mignon, so the revelers got down to the serious business of the feast. French champagne was ordered and brought over as livered waiters diligently filled slim crystal glasses with the sparkling liquid.

"At toast! A toast!" Frank Havens proclaimed, standing up from the table with his glass in hand. Each person took their own glass of bubbly and stood with him around the table. "To Mayor Rogers, and his lovely wife, Dottie, for their generous company this evening and to celebrate four more years of his able administration of our city."

"Here! Here!" Chief Hayes added.

With the toast done congratulations were given to the man of honor by all around that large table. Other diners at the Stork Club stood up and cheered as well, for the Mayor was a popular man, and a consummate politician.

However, one of the men who stood there drank rather slowly, almost carefully, his mind in deep thought and turmoil. Richard Curtis Van Loan could not help thinking about the Mayor's earlier words regarding his alter ego, The Phantom, and the fact that he would order his police to seek out the masked avenger and discover his secret identity. That could be a disaster, perhaps even a death sentence for The Phantom and for Van Loan.

Van looked over at the lovely visage of Muriel Havens, caught her eyes as she returned to him an inviting smile. A smile he could not return with the promise of anything more than mere friendship. Van Loan was in love with Muriel, but that love must remain unrequited on his part. Even though love for her flared blazing hot within him, it resided there from afar. So it would always be; so it must be. To do anything else, to declare his love for Muriel, to offer her marriage as he wished to do, to create a home and children, were all things Van Loan yearned for more than any other thoughts in his life except he had chosen another path. To live his life with Muriel would place her in terrible jeopardy and he could not do that to her.

Van sat down now, as did the other guests. They chatted amiably, eating, drinking, while he sat quiet, thoughtful. Since he had come back from The Great War, something had changed in the dashing young playboy. His time in the Army on the Western Front, in the air as a flyer, a "war bird," had transformed the wealthy young gadabout into a much more serious young man. He was a man to whom war had shown the futility of his rich and pampered life. When Van Loan, or Van as he was often called by his friends these days, came home from the war, he found peace time adjustment impossible. He craved action and adventure, danger and the exhilaration it brought him, but that was not to be in civilian life. He found himself lost back then, going through dark days, but on his darkest day his best friend Frank Havens, knowing of his troubles, came to him with a plan. A plan that promised the action and adventure he craved but could also be good for the people of the city he loved. Thus The Phantom was born.

"Van? Van, did you hear what I said?"

Van Loan looked up, smiled shyly, "Oh, sorry, Frank, I was just thinking about things."

"No doubt. You were pretty deep there. Listen, after this is over we need to talk," Havens informed him.

"Sure thing, Frank."

The evening wore on. Van Loan was in a dark mood over the news about the impending police action against The Phantom. He knew how things worked in this town. New policies like this were often first broached at dinners such as this one, just "table talk" ostensibly, among the movers and shakers to see how it went over with the swells. However, he knew that days or weeks from now, the official policy or rules would go into effect. Van knew the clock was running. He had no doubt that the police would soon put into effect a policy to capture The Phantom Detective. It heralded danger and concern but Van remained at the dinner despite these qualms. He even managed a dance with Muriel, the first time the two of them had been alone and in each other's arms in weeks.

The orchestra played a slow romantic tune and Richard Curtis Van Loan held Muriel Havens to him firmly as he effortlessly glided her across the dance floor. The rhythm was perfect, the beat of the music pulsing with romance, the lights over the dance floor warm, colorful, inviting. As were Muriel's luscious eyes and red lips.

"Oh, why don't we dance like this all the time, Van?" Muriel blushed, as she rested her head dreamily upon his broad shoulder.

"I missed you, you know that," Van Loan admitted, then instantly regretted his voicing even this minor indication of his affection.

"You say you do, Van, but you only come around to see my father, never me. Why?"

"Your father and I have serious business to attend to, and well…"

"Well, what, Van?"

He remained silent. They quickly turned, glided down the dance floor towards their table. The song was ending and so was the dance.

"What, Van? Tell me? Can you tell me at least that you love me?"

Richard Curtis Van Loan stopped in mid-stride. He held Muriel to him tightly, looked deeply into her eyes, she could feel his passion, but he said not a word. Nor did his lips meet hers as both of them so wanted.

"Tell me, Van. Please."

Van Loan so dearly wanted to tell the woman in his arms how much he loved her, how his very soul yearned for her, but he dared not. Finally he said softly, "All I can tell you is that I would never do anything to place you in danger, Muriel. And that is all I can say for now."

She allowed a tiny smile to escape her lips but she was obviously very disappointed by his remark.

The dance was over. The couples broke apart and returned to their seats. Muriel Havens dabbed at her eyes, there seemed to be some wetness there she could not control, so she asked to be excused and left for the Ladies Room with Dottie Rogers, the wife of the Mayor in tow.

With the women gone the men started talking business, politics, men things. It had been a long evening and a not very enjoyable one for Van

Loan but for his dance with the lovely Muriel; a memory he would always treasure.

Van Loan yawned and stretched loudly, "I fear the hour is getting late for me, my friends, I am afraid that I must offer up the poor excuse of fatigue to leave this wonderful gathering and head on home."

All there asked him to reconsider, to stay longer, but Van would not relent, he had made his decision to leave.

Van knew his driver, Rodney, would have the town car ready to bring up to the entrance as soon as he saw him out front of the building. Then he would make his getaway.

Van Loan addressed those at the table, "I offer you all a heartfelt good-bye and goodnight and thanks for a wonderful evening. Frank please say goodnight for me to Muriel, and the Mayor's wife, I am afraid I must be off."

The Mayor and many of the others at that table were a bit surprised that such a young wealthy playboy like Van Loan would be the first one to leave the party, but they allowed him to exit with their regrets. Van Loan thanked them all again, shook hands and then left the dining area.

Outside on the steps of the Stork Club Van lit a cigarette, inhaling the smoke in a deep breath of utter relaxation. He was finally by himself and alone. He looked down the street and saw the sleek black town car coming towards the curb of the club entrance. It was Rodney with his car.

"Hey, Boss," Rodney said with his usual smile. He was a stocky black man who had worked for Van Loan since he'd been a teenager, the two men were stalwart friends.

Van got into the front seat beside Rodney, "Just drive around."

"Sure thing," Rodney answered as he put the large luxury sedan into gear. Rodney knew Van Loan as a boss and as a friend. Sometimes the two relationships melded together. When Van sat up front in the car like he did now, Rodney knew his friend had things on his mind that he needed time to get sorted out. Rodney understood. He kept quiet, saying not a word, offering not a sentence, until Van decided he wanted to talk. Rodney knew that's the way his boss and friend was. He knew about the fancy dinner inside the Stork Club, with all them high muckaty-mucks, the Mayor and who knew who else and that Muriel Havens had to be there too. Rodney shook his head in dismay, wondering for the hundredth time why his friend didn't take that sweet young thing to wife like he wanted to.

"Ah, Boss?"

"Yes, Rodney? Sorry, rough night."

"That Miss Muriel was there, eh?"

"Yes," Van said dreamily.

"You're breakin' your heart over her."

"I know."

"Okay, Boss, just so you know. I'll be quiet now and keep driving 'til you tell me to stop."

"Thanks, Rodney."

Rodney drove the luxurious town car four hours, saying not another word to the silent man at his side. Rodney mused how the boss could sure get moody at times, but then again, he had a lot on his mind.

They drove down to the Battery and over the Brooklyn Bridge into Brooklyn. Rodney guided the luxury car down Flatbush Avenue, passed by Juniors Restaurant, he sure would have loved to stop and pick up some of that delicious cheesecake they were so famous for, but he knew this wasn't the right time for that. He continued driving up Flatbush towards Grand Army Plaza, drove around the circle passing the Museum and the Main Public Library, then headed back down Flatbush Avenue. That's when he saw it.

"Wow, Boss, check out that red flashing light atop the *Clarion* Building!"

"I see it. Take me there now."

Richard Curtis Van Loan looked ahead through the front window of the car and saw the skyscrapers of Manhattan. One of them, the tall art deco monument to wealth and power was the *Clarion* Newspaper Building, the tower at the top of which shone with a bright flashing red light, it was the summons for the Phantom Detective!

"Step on it, Rodney. Get me to the *Clarion* Building right away."

Rodney stepped on the gas and the huge car took off.

• • •

When Richard Curtis Van Loan arrived at the *Clarion* Newspaper Building he immediately went up the private elevator to publisher, Frank Havens', office. Havens was still there, seated at his desk. It had been almost five hours since Van Loan had left the Mayor's dinner at the Stork Club; obviously Havens had dropped off his daughter home, but had not stayed home himself. It was the middle of the night, yet Havens was here in his office and he had put out the call to The Phantom.

"What is it, Frank?"

"Van, we need to talk about the Mayor and Chief Hayes' plan to capture you, I mean The Phantom, and to discover his secret identity. We are en-

"...it was the summons for the Phantom Detective!"

tering dangerous waters here. Something doesn't seem right to me about this. Why all the interest now? Why has Mayor Rogers changed his policy all of a sudden? Something else has me worried. We don't want to have to fight the police on this, they'll be after you soon, you know what that could mean."

"I've been thinking about that. If it comes to having a shoot out with the cops. You know I would never do that, Frank."

"But things have a habit of getting out of control real fast sometimes; bullets fly, people get hit, hurt, even die, Van."

"So you want me to lay off for a while?" Van Loan asked his friend, unable to hide the disappointment in his voice.

"Hell no, Van! I don't want you to stop. I want you to move ahead on this on all cylinders, show them just what The Phantom can do. Show them all how valuable you really are."

"All right, I'm game, Frank, but that's a tall order," Van replied. "What should I do? Where do I start?"

"Well, that's the question, isn't it? The Mayor and Chief Hayes were doing some squawking about Big Nose Marino. Suppose you brought him in? Or suppose, you stopped one of his crime schemes, or even caught him at it? That would be just the thing."

"I could do that, or at least give it a look, but the man's clean as far as anyone knows," Van stated.

"He's not clean, take my word for it," Havens replied. "He just hasn't been brought down yet. He's smart, slippery, but his time may have come."

"Well Mayor Rogers seems almost obsessed with him," Van offered thoughtfully. "Something ain't right there."

"I agree, Van."

"I think there's more to things than meets the eye between them. Do you think the Marino mob is pressuring the Mayor?"

"Not sure, Van. Marino is a smart operator, don't let that big nose and his rough looks fool you, under that brutish appearance is a crook as slick as Al Capone and ten times as dangerous."

"I'll look into it, Frank."

"Good luck, Van. Keep me appraised of how things go."

• • •

Albert "Big Nose" Marino ran a gang that controlled crime in the city for years, but he'd always managed to stay out of things, and out of the newspapers. He'd never been fingered by a crook. He'd never been arrested, never seen the inside of a jail cell, but he seemed to be involved in a lot of what went wrong in the city. It was rumored he had his fingers in every crime that went on and that all criminals kicked back a portion of their scores to him. Or so it was whispered in certain circles, however nothing was ever proven.

Next morning, Van Loan began his investigation and went to have a talk with ace *Clarion* crime reporter Steve Huston. From Huston he learned the interesting fact that Albert "Big Nose" Marino, the man hated that moniker, had been one of the major financial contributors to Mayor Rogers re-election campaign.

"They're not buddies, Van," Huston told the wealthy playboy, "but there is a connection somewhere, I'm sure. He's given money to the Mayor, but no one knows how much. I think it might be considerable. I wish I could find the canceled checks. I'm surprised you don't know Marino, you both being rich and all, but I guess you don't move in the same circles he does,"

"Hardly, Steve," Van Loan offered, feigning arrogance with his tart reply.

"So what's your interest in Marino?"

"Just doing some background work for an article on city politics. Frank asked me to write up something for the paper on the wealthy society set and their interest in local politics," Van Loan said, offering up what seemed a logical answer to Huston's question.

"Well, then, you're the right guy for that. Rich playboy, old money, polo and politics, eh? Only be careful what you write about this guy, he's into more than polo."

"Thanks, I will. So can I borrow your Marino file?"

"Sure, here it is. It's a lot of stuff, I even have some FBI info, all raw data you understand, uncorroborated, but it might give you some ideas," Huston told him handing over the pile of papers and reports.

"Thanks, Steve, this is just what I need."

• • •

There was to be no article of course, but Van Loan now had what he wanted, a load of information on Big Nose Marino and all his numerous business ventures. Most were legal of course, but some...? Let's just say there were questions that Van would have liked to have answered. It was a big file, three inches thick, full of all kinds of material. It took Van two full days to read it all and digest all that he had read but it made interesting reading. He began reading it Tuesday morning and by Thursday night when he finished the file he felt he knew more about Marino than any man in town other than the man himself.

Van didn't worry about the lateness of the hour when he placed his call to Frank Havens. He knew the *Clarion* publisher would still be in his office and at his desk, probably working on getting out the bulldog edition.

"Van, where have you been, old boy? Havens asked, ignoring the lateness of the hour.

"Catching up on my reading."

"Ah, yes, Steve Huston told me you asked for his Marino file. Find anything?"

"I think so. I have a hunch, it's just a hunch, but it makes me kinda sick. I'm going to look into it. What I need to know is if there is a record of any scheduled appointments between Marino and the Mayor?"

"How would I know that, Van?"

"Put your people on it. You have someone in the Mayor's office, don't you?"

"Ah, well, yes I do."

"Good. Can you get him to take a look at the Mayor's appointment book?"

"*She* can give it a try. I'll call her now, then get back to you on it."

● ● ●

It was two days later when the phone rang at the Long Island estate of Richard Curtis Van Loan.

"Call for you, Boss," Rodney told him, bringing the phone out to the wrought iron table on the veranda where his employer was having breakfast.

Van Loan put the phone to his ear and heard a familiar voice. "Van, that you?"

"Yes, Frank, what can I do for you?"

"I'm worried, you know that thing you asked me for a couple of days ago?"

"Yes, the appointment book."

"Just so. Well, I told our gal there, Patty Day, to take a sneak look and call me back, she's one of the Mayor's secretaries but she used to work here at the *Clarion* for me."

"How convenient."

"Not so convenient. She's turned up missing."

Van jumped up alert now, "You sent someone around to her place?"

"I have some cops on the payroll, they did a search. Her apartment is empty, nothing mussed with, no sign of violence. But no one's seen her. It's like she just fell off the planet," Havens replied fearfully. "If that poor girl got hurt because of me I'll never forgive myself, Van."

"The Phantom will look into it right away, Frank."

• • •

City Hall was dark and quiet when the man in the dark suit and slouch hat with the black silk mask across his eyes entered Mayor Rogers' private office. The Mayor, of course, was not there this time of night but the masked man who silently entered was not there to see the Mayor at all, he wanted to get a look at a certain appointment book that was said to always be set in a particular spot upon the Mayor's desk. The Phantom startled, looked carefully upon the desk, but he could not find the book. It was not there!

Suddenly a sharp light shone upon him, it was a flashlight held in the hand of a dark figure off in the corner behind the door. Van had not seen the man when he'd entered the office, but the man had seen him. In one hand the mysterious intruder held the flash and what looked like the appointment book that he was desperately seeking; in the other hand the man held a gun pointed directly at Van Loan.

"This what you're looking for, fella?"

Van froze, saw the gun, knew he had fallen into a trap.

"Mr. Marino figured you'd be here after it, fella. So you're The Phantom? I expected someone who'd come in here with a gun out and ready for action. You have a gun, don't you?"

"I do. I only use it when necessary."

"You do, eh?"

"You'll find out soon enough," Van promised, angry with himself at having allowed this two-bit thug to get the drop on him and get his grubby hands on the appointment book.

"Yeah, that's what they all say, but I'm the one holding the gun, fella," the intruder declared boldly."

"For now. For now," Van answered forcefully. "So who are you? I can't see your face. You work for Big Nose Marino."

"The Boss doesn't like that moniker."

"Too bad, let me get a better look at you." Van said slowly walking toward the man.

"Stay back, I warn you! I got a gun, and I wouldn't mind being known as the man what shot and kilt the mysterious Phantom."

"Hah!" If that's so, you would have shot me long ago. You're under orders, my friend. What's the order?" Van asked boldly, his eyes focusing on the man's hands. In one hand he held the flashlight and the book, in the other the gun pointed at The Phantom. Van could see the man's hands were full, he was nervous, but also he was bold and cocky. That might be his undoing.

"The Boss wants me to bring you to him. He wants to talk," the man said.

"I'll bet," The Phantom replied grimly.

"You got a gun, take it out slow and careful, throw it down to the floor," the man ordered.

The Phantom smiled, he knew he could easily take this thug down, overpower him almost at will, but perhaps the best action now might be inaction; to allow himself to be taken captive and then brought to Big Nose Marino. Perhaps.

Deftly Van drew out his .38 and dropped it to the floor as ordered.

"Any other weapons?" the man demanded.

"No," The Phantom replied with a smirk.

The thug allowed a grim smile, "Sure. Turn around, I'm going to give you a pat down. I've got my pistol to your head so don't make a move. Try any funny stuff with me, fella, and I'll shoot, orders or no orders, understand?"

"I understand."

The man did not find any other weapons on The Phantom. He seemed satisfied that Van Loan was helpless and in his power and quickly lead him towards the door to exit the Mayor's office.

Now was the time.

In a sudden burst of fury The Phantom acted. One instant all seemed calm, the next second The Phantom's slouch hat was pulled off and pushed into the face of his captor obstructing his vision: while his other hand grabbed at the man's gun wresting it out of his hand. The man shouted in muffled rage, the slouch hat still pressed against his face obscuring his voice and vision. The thug dropped the book and his flashlight immediately, then bent over in pain as Van's fist sunk deep with a punch into his gut. For one second the thug was incapacitated and that's all it took. Van now had the gun and used it to smash the man over the head with a sharp whack from the barrel that sent him unconscious.

Now The Phantom got to work. He ignored the unconscious thug for the moment, pocketed the intruder's gun and retrieved his own .38. Then he picked up the flashlight and used it to look over the pages inside the appointment book. This was the book that Patty Day had gone missing over. Van only hoped the young lady had not been murdered my Marino's henchmen for what she had seen written in that book. As Van looked through the pages he noticed various appointments between Marino and Mayor Rogers. That was most curious. The two had been together numerous times. Then he noticed the words written in the margins by the Mayor about topics of conversation, and amounts of money paid. Campaign contributions or payoffs? Van could not be sure which. Then he came upon the note for an appointment last week, just a couple of days before the dinner at the Stork Club. The words he saw written there bore into Van's vision as the light from the flash played upon them. He read them once silently, then once out loud.

"'Marino wants the Phantom dealt with right away!'" Van repeated what the notation told him. "Damn!"

"So you want The Phantom dealt with, do you, Big Nose?" Van whispered to himself softly with grim menace. "Well, I want you dealt with, too!"

The Phantom knew that the connection between the Mayor and Marino was solid now, the book gave evidence of that for sure, but what exactly did it mean? How deep did the corruption go? He knew he'd have to get the truth out of Mayor Rogers and Big Nose Marino, but first he had to find and save the girl, Patty Day. To do that he had to rouse the intruder at his feet and question him. He had already tied up the man, so he was securely bound, and it appeared that he was slowly coming around back to consciousness. Van flashed the bright light upon his face.

"Wake up, sleeping beauty."

"Who...What?"

"Tell me, who are you?" Van demanded, making sure the man got a look at the .38 he held pointed directly at him.

"I'm not talking, fella."

"Oh, you'll talk. See, I'm holding the gun now, and you know what that means?"

"Don't know, fella."

"The Phantom, to you, *fella*," Van growled menacingly, repeating that last word in the exact voice and tone as the man had done a second before. Not mocking him, but in perfect mimicry. The Phantom was a master of mimicry. He was a man who could hear a voice just once and then imitate it perfectly. He also had amazing talents with make-up and impersonation; he was very skilled at the actor's art. The Phantom was also well-versed in the talents of ventriloquism and hypnotism. He could make-up his face and change it into an exact replica of his enemy. That talent, along with being able to ape the features, voice, and appearance of any enemy made him a success on infiltrating criminal gangs. He prepared to do that now as he carefully looked over his prisoner. He had already noted the man's appearance, his clothing, memorized his stance, his walk, his language. He already had the man's voice down pat, could imitate it perfectly.

"Now the last thing I need from you is the location of Patty Day," The Phantom demanded.

"Not telling ya, fella. The Boss would have my head if I do."

"I'll have your head if you don't."

"Come on, fella, I'm just doing a job here, I didn't even get paid yet," the man admonished the masked giant who stood over him.

"Then you should talk to me, you don't owe Marino anything," Van Loan argued. "Look, *fella*, I'll get it out of you one way or the other. It's of no consequence to me to kill another of Marino's henchmen, but there's another way. There's a way you could come out on top of this with a nice bundle of cash. Interested?"

The thug's eyes lit up with undisguised avarice and desire. No bullet, but some cash; now that made sense to him.

"I'm listening."

"Tell me what I want to know," Van Loan asked as he slowly pulled a wad of bills out of his pocket. They were all twenties, a lot of them, and the thug's eyes lit up just as Van knew they would.

"Well, I might consider..." he said as he licked his lips.

The Phantom peeled off the bills one at a time, teasingly slow, allowing them to float down to the floor in front of the helpless bound man. The man could not reach the bills to grab them up, but he certainly tried. The Phantom kept peeling the wad until it was gone and the floor of the Mayor's office around the thug was covered in a veritable carpet of twenty-dollar bills. The money meant nothing to a wealthy man like Van Loan, but he was well aware that it could be useful in loosening the tongue of most criminals.

"Your choice, start talking, *fella*," Van Loan ordered. "Then the cash is yours."

"Sure, I'll talk. Name's Charlie Stack. I was hired out of Jersey, you know, out of town talent, they calls it in the trade. Never thought I'd be under the power of The Phantom. You sure got the real guts, I'll give you that, and you know how to make a fella talk."

"So talk. Where's the girl, Patty Day?"

"Marino's got her at the old Anderson factory out in the Bronx. The place was abandoned years ago and he uses it as his headquarters."

"Tell me about the girl," Van demanded.

"The Mayor and Marino was having a meet when they caught her looking through the appointment book. Marino had me put the bag on her before she got home. They're holding her 'til she talks. She's a tough broad, won't spill. That's good for her because they want to find out what she knows before they kill her, but once she spills, she's done for," Charlie Stack told The Phantom with a crooked smile.

"You lie to me about any of this Charlie and I'll be back for you."

"I ain't lying, I swear," his smile fading away.

"All right, Charlie, I'm going to leave you now. When you get loose, or when someone sets you loose, pick up your cash and go back to Jersey and don't ever let me see you here in New York again."

"Yeah," Stack mumbled, "all right, Phantom."

"You understand, Charlie? I'm not playing, *fella*," The Phantom told him with grim menace in his voice as he allowed him to get another meaningful look at his .38.

"I understand," Charlie Stack admitted nervously.

"Good, now there's just one other thing I need."

"Yeah?"

"Your clothes."

• • •

The small swift roadster took Richard Curtis Van Loan through Manhattan and into the Bronx and finally to the old Anderson factory. Once, a decade before, the place had been a huge munitions plant humming with jobs and work for the war effort. Today it stood desolate and deserted. Or perhaps, not deserted. It was the perfect place for a crook master like Big Nose Marino to make his secret headquarters.

Van Loan drove up to the building slowly, passed by it noticing every inch of the place, then stopped his vehicle two blocks away. The area was dark and desolate. He turned off the engine and lights. Everything was quiet and deserted.

Now The Phantom got to work.

Van Loan took off his slouch hat and his silk mask. Then he took out his special black make-up box and used the various sticks of grease paint to change his face into that of the thug Charlie Stack. Van Loan painted his

"I'm not playing…fella!"

face, fixed his hair, used wadded up cotton balls to puff out his cheeks just like Stack's, used more cotton under the upper lip in his mouth to fill out his face. He added mixes of grease paint for more color and depth, knowing that in the dark, or the dim light, his face would be a good enough match for Charlie Stack's. Then Van got out of the car and got dressed in the thug's clothing. Now Van Loan was no longer The Phantom, he was just a two-bit thug from Jersey named Charlie Stack who worked for Big Nose Marino. Van Loan looked like Charlie, walked like Charlie, was dressed in Charlie's clothes, and when he spoke…

"That's it for you, fella! I sound just like you."

Richard Curtis Van Loan smiled at the impersonation. It was perfect. Now he began walking towards the Anderson factory, and his destiny.

When Van reached the huge metal door to the building he knocked twice loudly, waited, then knocked again.

"Hold on!" he heard a rough voice shout from inside. "I'm coming."

The heavy door was opened with a resounding groan from the rubbing of rusty metal against metal. A tall man with a gun stood defiantly in the doorway just hoping it was someone who would challenge him. He took one look at the newcomer, recognized him instantly, then nodded, "Okay, Charlie, the Boss is expecting ya, go on in."

"Thanks, fella."

Van Loan walked inside the deserted factory. The place was huge, but Van Loan saw a lighted area at the far end and made his way towards it. Once he reached the end of the factory floor he came upon a newly built section; there were tables, chairs, desks, and he saw a woman tied to a chair, apparently unconscious. Patty Day. Two gunmen stood guard.

"Charlie, glad you're back, boy. You got the book?" the big man behind the desk shouted in a victorious tone. He had a huge nose, and harsh brutish looks, but it was said they concealed a brilliant and deadly criminal mind so he knew he had to beware and play this all very carefully.

Van walked closer with careful deliberation. So far his disguise seemed to be working perfectly. He hoped it would last. He nodded slowly and pulled out the book from his coat pocket, "Yep, here it is, Boss."

Then he set the book down on Marino's desktop.

"Good work. I don't need to have my connections known with the Mayor. Certainly nothing written down like in this book. What about The Phantom? Did he show up?"

"I waited for him just like you told me to, Boss. He showed but wouldn't come with me so I had to drill him."

"So he's dead?"

"He's dead, Boss."

"Oh well, at least we have the book now. That's what I really wanted. And we still have the dame," Marino added, his eyes flitting to the woman bound in the chair.

"She talk yet, Boss?"

"No, she's playing it tough. I was waiting for you to get back, figured you could make her talk. I know how good you are at these sort of things, Charlie," Marino said with an evil leer.

Van looked over to the terror-stricken girl. Poor kid. Patty Day was securely tied to a chair, unable to move, she had a gag in her mouth but she was obviously alive, though scared to death. What she was hearing now about her fate made her even more frantic.

"Sure, Boss, but first there's something I have to do," then suddenly Van dropped all pretense of his impersonation and drew his .38 blazing away, first at the two guards dropping both of them instantly, then at Marino. Big Nose Marino saw the jig was up and frantically reached for a revolver in his desk drawer, but by the time he had it out, Van had his own .38 pointed squarely at Marino's head.

"Drop it, or I'll drop you!"

Big Nose Marino looked into the face of the man before him and wondered what the hell had happened. His two men were down. They looked dead. He had a gun pointed now at him. This surely wasn't Charlie Stack! Now that he looked at the man's face he noticed the eyes were all wrong, they had changed somehow. They were hard and sharp. Deadly. This man was not Charlie Stack at all; he was The Phantom in disguise!

Marino took a deep breath and lowered his gun in defeat. He knew better than to go up against such a merciless crime fighter as The Phantom, so he dropped his gun to the floor.

Quickly Van got to work. He tied up Marino, then released Patty Day. The woman was ecstatic with relief, she kissed him oozing her thanks. Van next checked on Marino's two goons, both of whom were dead. However he knew his time was slim, the shots would attract the big man over at the door, and he would be here soon to investigate with weapon drawn. Van moved off and found a good spot, then laid in wait for the guard quickly getting the drop on him, knocking him unconscious. That man was soon tied up and brought over to sit beside his boss.

"Now, Marino, I need some answers from you," Van Loan asked, purposely angling the light from the desk lamp into the gang bosses' eyes so he could not see the face of his captor. While Van was not wearing the Phantom's mask, the grease paint and lack of lighting went a long way in covering his true appearance. Van could see that Marino and his thug were having trouble seeing his face. That's just the way he wanted it.

Patty Day stood near the two men holding a gun on them that Van had taken from Marino and given to her for protection. Van then placed a phone call to the police giving them all the particulars, when he hung up he knew he didn't have much time before he would have to make his exit.

But first he had something else he had to do.

"I want answers now, Marino," Van Loan demanded.

"You're The Phantom!"

"I ask the questions now."

"Are you going to kill me?"

"I never kill anyone who doesn't deserve it."

That was not what the gangster lord wanted to hear.

"I want answers. Then what happens to you is your own accord. You kidnapped Patty Day, the police are on the way. I want to know what's your connection with the Mayor."

Marino shrugged, like it was a meaningless question, "Nothing, I gave him some money for his campaign. He didn't want it getting out in the newspapers, that's all."

"Money for special favors?" Van asked bitterly.

"What do you think smart guy?"

"Just what I figured. There's one more thing I want to know. Why the mention in the Mayor's appointment book of The Phantom? What was that about?"

Marino smiled, shrugged, "Oh, that? I can tell you that. It was my first favor due from the Mayor. Get The Phantom menace off the streets so I could operate my various business ventures with impunity. I realized right away that my cash could buy me political influence and that I could have the Mayor make the police do my dirty work for me. See, Phantom, I've been aware of you for months now. I know it was you who captured the gang I had rob the First National, and that kidnapping case? Those people are so rich! You quashed that scheme too for me. So I figured I needed to get you out of the picture and the best way to do that would be to have the cops themselves do it for me. Nice, eh? A few words spoken in the right ear at times can work wonders."

"So you bought the Mayor and had him order the Police Chief to capture The Phantom and have him proclaimed a menace and a criminal."

"Pretty good, eh? And it almost worked," Marino said proudly.

"Almost, don't count, Big Nose."

"Don't call me that!"

"I'll call you what I want to call you," Van growled.

Big Nose Marino suddenly grinned malevolently, "Okay, Phantom, no skin off my nose, there's always another day, and another way to get things done. By this time tomorrow I'll be out on bail, and even if I eventually somehow get a conviction in the Patty Day thing, he looked over at the woman and smiled innocently, I guarantee you it won't be more than an inconvenience to me. I'll be back Mr. Phantom, and then we'll see who the final winner of this competition is!"

"The cops are here," Patty Day announced suddenly. Men in dark blue uniforms and with guns drawn were now rushing into the building and running down toward them.

That was Van Loan's cue to get lost. Instantly he melted into the surrounding darkness and was gone. One minute later he was back in his roadster headed back downtown into Manhattan.

• • •

Mayor Rogers was in a private meeting with newspaper publisher Frank Havens at the latter's luxurious office in the prestigious *Clarion* Building. The two men were talking about The Phantom and the Mayor's recent decision to order the police to track down the masked man and discover his true identity.

"I'm telling you it's a bad decision, Mayor," Havens spoke firmly, and Rogers did listen patiently, for the newspaper magnet had a lot of pull in this city. A lot of pull, Havens realized, but apparently not as much as certain other people who seemed to exert severe influence over the Mayor these days.

"I'm sorry, Frank, I really am," Mayor Rogers said using the best political soft-soap voice that he had in his large repertoire, one he saved for his most influential constituents, "it's a decision I have to go through with. I have no choice."

"Well, I thought I would ask you up here one last time, friend to friend, to try to change your mind."

"And I appreciate that, Frank, and for your years of support," Rogers oozed smoothly.

"Then if you won't listen to me, there is just one other person I hope you will listen to, Mr. Mayor," Havens asked.

"I can't see how anyone else could change my decision," the Mayor stated firmly, then with a kindly smile added, "but you know me, Frank, I'm always willing to listen, at least."

"That's good to hear, Mayor," Havens said softly, hiding a wry grin. "Then I want to introduce you to another one of your constituents who would like to say a few words."

The Mayor nodded indulgently.

The door to Havens' office suddenly opened and in strode a shocking image. Mayor Rogers startled in his seat, for it was the masked crime fighter himself!

"The Phantom!" Rogers blurted fearfully now, utterly shocked.

The tall, well dressed man in black, wearing a large slouch hat and black silk mask across his eyes to conceal his identity walked towards where the Mayor was seated and plopped something down in his lap.

"What's this?" Rogers blurted, though he knew very well what it was.

"It's your appointment book, Your Honor. It details your association with Albert 'Big Nose' Marino and his criminal empire; an association that has now ended. Marino and his men have been arrested for the kidnapping and attempted murder of your secretary, Patty Day. She has been freed and is singing to the police and the FBI now," the masked man stated simply.

"I had nothing to do with that kidnapping business!" Rogers pleaded.

"But you knew all about it!" the masked man accused bluntly.

Mayor Rogers did not reply. He swallowed hard, nervous, his mind working fast, making sense out of all he had just heard and wondering how it could affect him. What was the worst case scenario? He realized all this could affect him severely. He grew more fearful, wondering just what the masked man before him knew.

"Marino will see prison for what he has done, and while I am sure you are guilty of corruption on a grand scale, I can not prove you had any involvement in the Day kidnapping, so you may have escaped that bullet, Mr. Mayor. Only one thing concerns me now. What I want to know is why you made that note in your appointment book about me and more so, what are you going to do about it now?" The Phantom said sharply.

Mayor Rogers swallowed hard, looked for encouragement and help towards Frank Havens, who only shook his head. He'd get no succor there, so he thought harder, deciding whether he should construct a suitable lie... or perhaps...even tell the truth.

"And you better tell me the truth," The Phantom blurted in anger, "because you don't know what I know."

Well, that did it. Mayor Rogers nodded, began slowly, "Marino and I were friends from youth, but as adults we had gone our separate ways. I stayed away from him, but for my re-election bid I needed money, and a lot of it; campaign contributions. I was involved in a tight election race. So Marino gave me the money I needed."

"And like everything he does, it comes with strings attached?" Frank Havens added.

"Yes, so I owed him," Rogers said starring at the grim visage of The Phantom standing before him. "No sooner was I re-elected than Marino comes to see me to collect. The note about you in my appointment book I put there because Marino wanted The Phantom out of the picture. I didn't understand it then, I even told him it didn't seem very important in the grand scheme of things, but he insisted. It was like he was obsessed with you. I couldn't tell you why, and he would not elaborate to me about it."

"I know why," The Phantom said starkly and the Mayor grew fearful.

"Why?" the Mayor asked nervously.

The masked figure before him did not answer.

"So what are you going to do now, Mr. Mayor?" Frank Havens interjected in a forceful tone, looking from Rogers over to The Phantom. "You know, what are you going to do to set things right, for our friend here?"

"I…I don't know…"

"Think hard, Mr. Mayor," The Phantom advised forcefully.

"Well, I am going to call Police Chief Hayes and tell him I have revoked my decision to label The Phantom as a menace and to have him captured?"

Frank Havens smiled, passed over the telephone. "That sounds about right. Here, you can make the call right now, use my phone."

Mayor Rogers made the call.

"Yes, Chief Hayes, that's correct, my order regarding The Phantom has been rescinded. Absolutely. Do not seek to arrest or capture The Phantom. We must not interfere with his noble work fighting against crime."

Frank Havens looked at The Phantom, his long-time friend Richard Curtis Van Loan, and gave him a victorious smile. "Well, I think that sets things on the correct path, don't you agree, Mr. Phantom?"

"Yes," The Phantom replied, "but I'm keeping your appointment book, for insurance. It may not be enough to convict you of a crime, but it sure will kill your political ambitions!"

Then the mysterious masked man left the room as suddenly as he had entered.

Mayor Rogers, who by now was sweating bullets finally muttered,

"Well, I'm certainly glad he's gone. I feel that my life may have actually been in danger from that man."

"Perhaps, Mayor," Frank Havens said sharply, "but there's just one more tiny item of unfinished business that we have today in this meeting."

"And what is that, Frank?"

Suddenly the door to Frank Havens office burst open and into the room strode wealthy socialite playboy Richard Curtis Van Loan. He immediately saw the Mayor with Havens and acted as if he was most upset at having intruded upon their private meeting.

"Oh! Frank, I'm so sorry, I didn't realize you had company. Hello, Mr. Mayor. I was in the building and thought I'd take a jaunt upstairs to see you, Frank, you know, see how things were shaking? I apologize at the intrusion; I'll take my leave right away."

"Hello, Van, no problem. Please stay. Come on in. I was just talking with the Mayor. Come on in, won't you? Join us."

Van Loan entered the large office, plopped down upon a elegant chair across from Mayor Rogers, all appearance of his alter ego as The Phantom now totally erased from his face and form. Instead there now sat the wealthy socialite playboy.

"So how are you these days, Mr. Mayor?" Van inquired innocently.

"Middling, Mr. Van Loan, middling. We just had a visit from that rogue, The Phantom"

"You don't say! The Phantom!" Van Loan exclaimed in mock shock. "Here?"

"Yes, right in this very room! It quite unnerved me, I must admit," the Mayor added. Obviously he was still recovering from the stress of his recent encounter with the masked crime fighter and his close brush with danger.

"That's true, Van," Havens added with a wry grin. "It was The Phantom himself. Quite shocking, let me tell you and he was able to convince the Mayor to rescind his order."

"I see," Van Loan stated. "Well, it may be for the best. Once again, I must apologize for bursting in on your meeting like this, I'm sure you and Mayor Rogers have a lot of important matters to discuss, Frank," Van Loan added.

"Well, actually, Van, we're just about finished here. There's just one last little thing that needs to be done."

The Mayor looked up at Frank Havens curiously.

"Mayor Rogers has to sign this letter. You see, he has decided that for

health reasons, he is going to resign his office as Mayor, effective immediately."

"I am!" Rogers blurted in surprised anger.

"For health reasons, Mr. Mayor, health reasons that have to do with The
Phantom. If you know what I mean?"

The Mayor shuddered in terror, "Ah, yes, quite right," Rogers stammered, quickly thinking things over and now shaking with fear once
again. "Are you sure he will he leave me alone if I resign my office?"

"I am certain of it," Frank Havens said softly. "Don't you think so, Van?"

"Absolutely. Once Mayor Rogers becomes law-abiding Citizen Rogers,
he is no threat to that terrible masked man. I tell you, it would simply ter-
rify me to know such a man was my enemy. Perhaps even after me? Don't
you agree, Mayor?"

"Yes, yes that is true. The man is a menace! Frank, where do I sign?"
Mayor Rogers blurted as he was shown where to put pen to paper and
duly signed his name resigning his office as Mayor of New York. After he
signed the letter and handed it to Frank Havens the former Mayor signed
deeply and stated, "It is done."

● ● ●

Frank Havens and Richard Curtis Van Loan sat alone in the newspaper
magnet's office, sharing drinks. One had a whisky sour and the other a
vodka with orange juice. Van Loan also enjoyed a cigarette.

"He was corrupt, even if we couldn't prove it to a certainty," Van Loan
offered. "He had to go."

"Yes, so it's best he went this way and is now gone," Havens added.

"There'll have to be a new election, of course," Van stated.

"But the main thing is that The Phantom is free to continue his work
and that's the most important thing of all, Van."

Richard Curtis Van Loan, alias The Phantom Detective leaned back
and nodded in relief, "It's good to know that I'll still be watching for that
flashing red light at the tower atop your building, Frank. The Phantom
Detective will continue his work."

"That's the ticket, Van, that's what I want to hear, after all, it's what you
do so well."

THE END

GARY LOVISI— is a Mystery Writer's of America Edgar Nominated author for his crime fiction. He is a fan, reader and collector of the classic pulp magazine stories and the classic authors, books and magazine. Lovisi has written stories featuring such iconic pulp heroes as The Crimson Mask, The Moon Man and The Purple Scar, all for Airship 27 publications. He is a big fan of Van Loan and The Phantom. Lovisi's latest books are two John Carter of Mars pastiche-type novels in his John Kirk of Ares pulp adventure SF series: The Invisible Men (#2) and The Space Men (#3) with books #4 and #5 out in 2017 from Wildside Press, (book #1 in the series, The Winged Men, appeared in 2014); and The Last Goodbye, hard pulp crime featuring tough guy Vic Powers (from Bold Venture Press). Lovisi is the founder of Gryphon Books, and the editor of Paperback Parade magazine. To find out more about him, his work, or Gryphon Books, visit him on Facebook and at his website: www.gryphonbooks.com.

Circle of Despair

by Gene Moyers

A taxi swerved to a stop in front of a tall apartment building on Park Avenue. Out stepped a tall, well groomed young man dressed in formal attire. He paid off the cab and pushed through the revolving door into the well-appointed lobby. As he crossed it he nodded to the doorman while tugging off his gloves and removing his top hat. The doorman stood up and waved to get his attention. Diverted from heading for the bank of elevators Richard Curtis Van Loan smiled at the approaching man. The uniformed employee touched the brim of his cap as he held out an envelope, "This was left for you earlier Mr. Van Loan." Van thanked the doorman and pressed a coin into his hand. Tearing open the letter, Van frowned as he read it. Slipping the letter into a pocket of his overcoat he reversed his course and reached the sidewalk seconds later. Fortunately a taxi was just letting out a fare.

Van Loan hopped into the taxi and ordered, "The *Clarion* building, and step on it." The cabbie dropped the flag and leaned on his horn as he swerved into traffic. In the back Van glanced at his watch; it was after ten thirty. If Frank Havens, owner and publisher of one of New York's most influential newspapers wanted to see him at this time of night it could mean only one thing: There was work for the Phantom Detective. Havens was the only man alive who knew that easy going man about town Dick Van Loan was the mysterious crime fighter the Phantom Detective. In fact, Havens had been instrumental in recruiting and helping Van develop his skills and become the Phantom. Van could only assume that a late night summons to Havens' office meant there was trouble afoot.

Minutes later the cab dropped Van in front of the *Clarion* building. He entered and took the elevator to the floor where Havens office was located. The receptionist had long left the building and Van knocked directly on the door marked *Private*. A voice bade him enter and Van opened the door to the private office of Frank Havens. The room was large and furnished more like a comfortable study than a newspaper office. The walls were covered in fine wood and there was a warm fire burning in the fireplace. As Van entered Havens stood up and came around his desk holding his hand out. Havens was a stocky, gray haired man of middle age with a dignified manner and intelligent face.

After shaking hands, Havens waved Van to a seat near the fireplace. Van took a seat on a comfortable sofa while Havens sat in a nearby armchair, "Thanks for coming so quickly Van. I appreciate it." Van waved a hand negligently, "I came as soon as I got your message. I would have come sooner if you'd used the light." Van was referring to the red light atop the *Clarion* building that was used to alert the Phantom Detective that he was needed urgently. Frank Havens looked a little uncomfortable at this, "I'm afraid this isn't the sort of thing you usually get involved in. In fact, it's a personal matter."

Van leaned back and raised an eyebrow, "Personal? How?"

"An acquaintance of mine, a friend actually, has died suddenly and I was wondering if you could look into it?"

Sobered Van spoke, "I'm sorry to hear that Frank. Who was it?"

Havens looked sad as he spoke, "His name was Rob Exley. He was a reporter for the *Post*. I've known him for nearly twenty years. I was just a reporter years ago when he started as a copy boy. We've both moved up since then of course. We've worked together or on rival papers but we've always stayed in touch. It was a shock to lose him so suddenly." Havens sat back, his gaze drifted away and Van let him lose himself in old memories. He cleared his throat before speaking, "And you think his death might have something to do with a story he was working on?"

Havens shook his head, "No. The police say it was suicide but I don't believe it for an instant." Havens went on to tell Van that Exley's body had been found in an alley behind his fifth floor apartment that morning. A search of his apartment by police had turned up no evidence of foul play and they were tentatively calling the death a suicide. Havens was doubtful of this and had called on Van hoping he could look into the matter. Van did not hesitate. He assured his old friend that he would investigate the reporter's death. He then wished Havens goodnight and left the office. He had no trouble locating a taxi to drop him back at his Park Avenue building.

After a quick breakfast Van looked over the day's newspaper. He found the one column story reporting the reporter's death on a back page. It offered nothing new. Entering his bedroom Van moved to his luxurious Empire style bed and found the hidden button behind it. He pressed it and silently a section of wall behind the bed opened revealing a hidden room. The lights came on automatically as Van moved into the windowless space.

Barely glancing about, he moved directly to a well-lit dressing table fronted by three mirrors. He did not even glance at the rest of the un-

usual room. On one wall was set up a compact but well equipped chemical laboratory. Another wall had racks of equipment and lockable cabinets containing an arsenal of varied weapons. There were also racks of
clothing containing everything from rags to formal wear. It was the secret
room where Dick Van Loan could transform himself into the Phantom
Detective.

Once at the table Van went to work. First he used a special cream to
slightly darken his complexion. Then using a variety of make-up pencils
he transformed his features. By clever work he added shadows under his
cheek bones to give him a slightly thinner face. He added coloring under his eyes to give the effects of bags under them. Finally he used a col-
or comb to carefully give himself graying temples and a dusting of gray
through the rest of his hair. He sat back to judge his appearance. The dashing millionaire clubman had vanished; in his place was a tired, middle
aged man. Van smiled. Perfect.

Next he moved to the wardrobe racks. He selected a decent but worn
brown suit and a cheap shirt and tie to match. When outfitted he judged
himself in the mirror to be the perfect image of an overworked, middle
aged police detective. From his arsenal Van selected a regulation police
.38 revolver that he holstered on his hip. He added his marvelous universal
master key in the jacket's right pocket and his detective bureau's badge
in the left. Adding a pocket flash he clapped a worn fedora on his head
and left the secret room. He closed the hidden door and made for his private elevator to the lobby. He then turned away from the lobby and exited
through a private entrance. As he did so he made sure that the tiny plati-
num domino mask that identified him to law enforcement was hidden in
his waistband.

Once on the street the Phantom walked briskly the few blocks to the
garage where he kept his stable of high powered cars. He nodded to Rogers
the garage owner as he entered. As the garage man was about to ask him
his business the Phantom reached across his chest with his right hand and
pulled the lobe of his left ear. This was the signal to those in the know that
the disguised stranger in front of them was the Phantom. Rogers quickly
returned the nod and said, "They're all ready to go sir. Which will it be?"

"I'll take the sedan." The Phantom crossed to the car, climbed in and
pressed the starter. Rogers nodded as the disguised socialite drove past
him. He had his own ideas about the mysterious disguised man but he was
well paid to keep his thoughts to himself. The Phantom expertly guided
his car uptown, west of Central Park. Locating the address that Havens

had given him he parked and went into the building. In the inner vestibule he pushed the bell labeled *manager* and waited. Soon a middle aged man appeared. He quickly admitted the Phantom when shown the detective bureau badge. Upon request he showed the Phantom to the fifth floor and unlocked Exley's apartment.

Once alone, the Phantom went quickly to work. The apartment was not luxurious but it was comfortable. The kitchen and living room were neat and held no interest for him. Exley's bedroom also held little of interest. A brief search there turned up nothing but clothes and personal items. The other bedroom had been turned into the reporter's study. A desk with a typewriter on it dominated the room. Two walls contained bookshelves. The other wall was covered with framed photos and documents. The window was closed but the drapes had been opened.

Moving to the window the Phantom bent and examined it closely. His keen eyes detected the residue of finger print powder. He nodded having expected this. He noticed nothing unusual. He turned the lock and lifted the sash. Leaning out the window he looked downward. There was no fire escape and nothing to stop a long fall to the darkened alley below. Using his flashlight the Phantom carefully examined the sill. He found nothing incriminating but his flashlight beam continued out and down. Leaning far out the Phantom carefully looked at the brickwork. The Phantom detected something and looked closer. He ducked back into the room and crossed to the desk. He quickly searched the drawers and soon came up with an unused envelope. Back at the window he opened a pocket knife and leaning out carefully scraped a small speck into the envelope.

After pocketing the envelope the Phantom looked around the room and frowned. He crossed to the wall of photos and scanned them carefully. There was Exley's college degree from the school of journalism issued by a Connecticut college that the Phantom recognized. There were also certificates of commendation and other journalistic awards. Moving down the wall there were photos: some clearly of family, others of professional friends, including one of Exley and Frank Havens together. One photo that the Phantom took note of was an obvious wedding photo of a younger Exley and bride. Standing back the Phantom looked at the whole wall and nodded to himself; something was missing.

He then moved to the bookshelf and looked carefully around. He ignored the obvious fiction volumes and instead made a careful perusal of a lower shelf that contained professional journals and reference books. He carefully fingered the space between two books then lifted out a photo album. Opening it he quickly flipped through the pages scanning the personal photos. He found the usual assortment of vacation, family and personal photos. What interested him most though were empty spaces that obviously had held photos that had been removed. He could feel the gum residue left behind when they had been pulled away. He replaced the album and quickly and thoroughly searched Exley's desk. He found nothing of interest, especially not the one thing he had been looking for. Thoughtfully he picked up the phone and dialed a number.

Frank Havens' private line rang. He picked it up and heard the voice of Dick Van Loan. "Hello Frank, I have a question for you. Rob Exley was married, where is his wife living?"

Careful to keep his voice neutral and not give any clues as to the Phantom's real identity he answered, "Rob and his wife Kate divorced a couple of years ago. They stayed friends though."

"Does she live here locally?"

"Somewhere in Brooklyn I believe. I'm not sure of the address though."

"Did she keep his name?"

"Yes, she did." The Phantom thanked Havens and rang off. He reached into a desk drawer and sorted through the directories. He located the one he wanted and a few minutes quick work gave him an address. Returning the directory to the drawer, he quietly exited the apartment. Minutes later he was guiding his powerful car across Manhattan toward the Brooklyn Bridge.

Once in Brooklyn he quickly located the modest apartment building where Kate Exley lived. A middle aged, attractive woman answered his knock. "Can I help you," she asked politely.

The Phantom flashed his detective badge, "Detective Gray, ma'am. I'd like to ask you a few questions about the death of your former husband."

The woman looked sad, "Of course. Please come in." Once in the tidy apartment its owner indicated an over-stuffed sofa. The Phantom sat. Before he could speak she said, "I don't know what else I can tell you. I told those other detectives everything I knew yesterday."

The Phantom nodded agreeably, "Just a few follow up questions, ma'am. Mr. Exley obviously knew many people. Did he have any friends that would know anything about his state of mind? Perhaps some long-time friends?"

Kate Exley hesitated a moment, "Well, there was Bill, Bill Pearce." She thought about it a minute, "And there was Dave Hayden."

"Had he known these men long?"

"Oh yes, He's known Dave since college and I think he's known Bill for nearly as long." After a few more questions the Phantom thanked her and took his leave. Before he left Brooklyn he stopped and made a phone call to the *Clarion's* editor. He asked Havens to have Steve Huston meet him at the Green Spot at one o'clock.

Once back in Manhattan the Phantom drove straight to his Park Avenue apartment. He parked around the corner and took his private entrance up to his suite. Once inside he made straight for the hidden room behind his bed. Removing the envelope from his pocket he carefully mounted the small particle onto a glass slide and slipped it onto the stage of a powerful microscope. It took no longer than a moment of focusing to confirm what the Phantom had suspected. It was definitely organic, probably skin cells. He frowned at the important evidence. Quickly leaving his secret room he left for his meeting.

Steve Huston's step was light and his mood good as he turned into the Green Spot. The tall, keen faced young man was an "ace" reporter for the *Clarion* and he had been thrilled when Frank Havens had told him of the meet today. He had worked with Phantom before, mostly doing leg-work but he felt that many times he had contributed significantly to the Phantom's successes against crime. As he pushed through the doors of the popular watering hole he was already looking around eagerly trying to recognize the Phantom. He moved toward the back room but the only occupant was a middle aged man having a beer. Huston pegged him as an off duty cop and was about to move on when the man's right hand went to his left ear.

Steve changed directions and pulling out a chair dropped into it opposite the Phantom. Shaking his head he spoke softly, "I am always surprised. I can never pick you out."

The Phantom smiled, "Good to see you Steve. Have a beer." He waved a hand at a waitress. Steve nodded and asked, "So what do you have for me today?"

"Frank Havens has asked me to look into Robert Exley's death."

Steve sobered, "I heard about that. Terrible."

"Did you know him?"

Steve shrugged, "Met him several times. He was a cracker-jack reporter. In fact he was up for the city editor's job over at the *Post*."

The Phantom noted that fact, "I need some information Steve. I need to find out what you can on a Dave Hayden and a Bill Pearce. They were supposed to be old friends of Exley's."

Steve looked sharply at the disguised figure, "Wasn't Exley's death a suicide?"

The Phantom held his gaze, "I'm having doubts. While you're at it ask around and see if you can find any other long-time friends of Exley's. Give anything you find to Havens; I'll get it from him."

Steve nodded as his beer was brought. The Phantom threw a bill on the table and quickly left. Once in his car he motored downtown. Twenty minutes later he was showing his detectives badge and being admitted to the coroner's office. The assistant coroner he spoke to was a harried, overworked man who barely remembered Exley's autopsy. Fortunately the Phantom had only one question for him, "Were the deceased's fingertips injured?"

The busy doctor replied absently, "The man fell five stories. There were a lot of injuries, but yes his fingertips were abraded." Thanking him, the Phantom took his leave. He returned his car to the garage and then went back to his apartment. Having removed his current disguise he spent the remainder of the evening thinking, making phone calls and considering possibilities.

Late the next morning a special messenger delivered a package to Dick Van loan at his apartment. It was from Havens. Tearing it open Van found a concise report from Steve Huston. It listed his recent friends, mostly fellow journalists and gave details on the two people Van had inquired about. Dave Hayden was an accountant employed by the Federal Reserve at their New York office. William Pearce was a municipal judge. They both had known Exley since college. Hayden lived in Manhattan, Pearce on Long Island. Their addresses were included. Huston closed with word he was still looking into Exley's past.

Sipping his coffee Van mused that that was why Pearce's name had seemed so familiar. He had read somewhere recently that he was being appointed to the circuit court soon. Throwing off his dressing gown Van moved briskly into his bedroom, opened his secret room and went to work.

A half hour later he emerged from the side entrance to his building again having taken on the appearance of detective Gray. Once in his car he drove downtown and parked near the Federal Reserve building. His detective's badge got him inside and he requested to see Mr. Hayden. A few minutes later a thin, well dressed, scholarly looking man came to meet him. The Phantom showed his badge and spoke, "I'd like to ask you a few questions about Robert Exley."

Hayden looked sad, "It was a terrible losing Rob like that. What can I do to help detective?"

"How long did you know him?"

"Over twenty years now. We went to college together."

"And you stayed close?"

"Yes. We kept in touch. We both lived here in the city so we saw each other fairly regularly."

"Do you know if anyone would have wanted to harm him?"

Hayden looked surprised, and then thoughtful, "No. Why would anyone have wanted to harm Rob?"

"That's what I'm trying to find out. Had you seen any change in him lately?"

Hayden seemed confused, "Changed? Changed how?"

"Did he seem worried? Perhaps he was depressed?"

Hayden shook his head, "I spoke to him last week. He didn't sound depressed then."

"He seemed normal to you?"

"Well, he sounded tired. Probably work. He was often on a hot story."

The Phantom wrote something on his note pad and nodded, "Did you know that he was about to be promoted to city editor?"

Hayden looked surprised, "Uh, no I didn't." The Phantom thanked the accountant and left. He then motored the short distance to the municipal court building. He located the court room where Judge Pearce was presiding and slipped into a back row to listen to the proceedings. Soon enough Judge Pearce called a recess for lunch and the court room emptied. The Phantom again used his badge to gain access to the judge's chambers. He knocked and was admitted. Judge Pearce was a large, rapidly graying man of perhaps forty years of age. He was just putting on his suit coat and hat, "I'm sorry, I'm just leaving for lunch."

Hat in hand the Phantom apologized, "Sorry your honor. Detective Gray, I just have a couple of questions concerning a death."

The judge stopped and looked at his watch, "I can give you a couple of minutes Detective. What do you need?"

"You were friends with Robert Exley?"

The judge looked pained, "Yes. I knew him since school, a terrible tragedy him taking his own life."

The Phantom nodded, "Can you tell me if he was under any strain lately or was he worried about anything?"

The judge looked closely at the disguised detective before replying carefully, "If you're looking for a motive for suicide, I couldn't say. Although I do know he took his divorce hard. He was also working very hard. Newspaper work is high stress, you know."

The Phantom nodded again, "Did you speak to him often?"

Again there was the slightest hesitation, "Not as often as I should have apparently. We have drifted apart recently."

The Phantom flipped his notebook closed and reached for the door handle, "I think that's all. Thank you for your time, your honor." The judge nodded. As he left the office he looked back and said, "One more thing. Where did you go to college your honor?" The judge looked surprised, "I went to Evergreen State College in Connecticut, but I took my law degree at Columbia. Why do you ask?"

"Just curious. Thank you." As he left the building the Phantom thought to himself; Judge Pearce was good at covering his emotions but not good enough. He was certainly holding something back. What was more interesting was the fact that the judge had attended Evergreen State College. Rob Exley had had a college diploma from the same college on his wall.

Deciding that he needed to know more about these two friends of Exley, the Phantom staked out Hayden's apartment that evening. It was in a decent Westside neighborhood. Hayden arrived home just after six and never left that evening. Deciding that the accountant was staying in that night, the Phantom finally gave up and went home at eleven.

The next day Van did more research at home. He made a few calls, the most interesting to Evergreen State College. Posing as a prospective employer it was easy to get the registrar to confirm that Hayden was indeed also a graduate of the college.

That afternoon the Phantom, once again wearing his detective Gray disguise, drove his car to Long Island. By five o'clock he had located the house of Judge Pearce and scouted the neighborhood. Although certainly not a mansion, it was a good sized house on a large tree covered lot. Parked in a spot where he could clearly see the house the Phantom waited.

Darkness fell and no lights came on in the house. Either the judge was unmarried with no servants or his family was away today. At nine o'clock the Phantom had just about decided that the evening would be as unproductive as the night before when car headlights turned into the block. He ducked low in his car and watched a sedan pull into the judge's driveway. He sat up and watched the house. Lights came on downstairs.

After some time the Phantom left his car and crept toward the house. Circling it he looked in the lighted windows. He found the judge eating a solitary dinner in the kitchen. Soon he finished and left the room. Moving around the house he found the judge had entered what appeared to be his study. He sat at a desk and began writing. The Phantom faded back to his car and continued to wait.

"The Phantom staked out Haven's apartment..."

By ten o'clock he decided on another check of the house. He found the judge still in his study but now he was sitting at his desk drinking a brown liquid from a large snifter. Shaking his head the Phantom prepared to withdraw when the judge glanced at his watch. Looking thoughtful he reached into one of the desk drawers and pulled out a revolver. He flipped open the cylinder and checked the chambers then closed it and replaced it in his desk. Certain now that the evening was going to get interesting the Phantom slipped back to his car.

At ten thirty the lights of a car approached. It parked down the street and the lights were extinguished. Soon a figure approached the house. From what he could see the Phantom made out a stocky figure wearing an overcoat and hat. He knocked at the front door and after a moment was admitted.

Approaching the house himself the Phantom circled it looking for the judge and his guest. He could not see them but noticed that the shade of the study had been pulled down. Frowning he crept below the window and listened. The sill was just above ear level and at first he could only hear the murmur of muffled conversation. Soon though, the words grew louder. He heard one voice saying something about a threat. There came a reply that was too low for the Phantom to make out. Suddenly a shot rang out, then another.

Drawing his pistol the Phantom sprinted around the house to the front door. It was locked. He rammed his shoulder against it. The door rattled violently but held. Realizing it was too strong to break he pointed his gun at the lock and fired twice. The lock shattered and the door crashed open when the Phantom gave it a violent kick. He rushed into a hall brightened only by light coming down the stairs. Darkened rooms lay to his right and left. Ahead, light came from open doors toward the rear of the house. From out of a doorway halfway down the hall a stocky figure in an overcoat rushed firing a pistol in the Phantom's direction. He ducked and fired his revolver in return. Rather than fighting, the figure backpedaled down the hall firing as he went. The Phantom managed another shot but was unsure of his aim as the figure disappeared into what looked like the kitchen.

Dashing down the hall the Phantom paused for a moment to glance into the study. He took in the limp form of Judge Pearce on the floor before he continued pursuit. The kitchen was empty and the back door was open. Pausing by the back door, he flipped off the overhead light so he wasn't silhouetted and leaped through the back door and off the porch. Only silence greeted him. The Phantom sprinted around the house and cut across lawns toward where he had seen the visiting car park. As he neared the street he heard an engine start. By the time he reached the street the gunman's car was too far away for a shot. He watched its tail lights dwindle and disappear.

Returning to the house the Phantom entered. All was quiet. Apparently none of the neighbors had heard the shots. In the study the Phantom confirmed that the judge was dead. He had been shot twice. Interestingly a drawer was open and his revolver was lying on the rug. So the judge had tried to draw it at some point during the argument. The Phantom looked for the note or letter that the judge had been writing earlier. He found the pad and fountain pen but the letter was gone. Had the unknown assailant taken it? Thinking back he thought he remembered the gunman with something in one hand as he fled.

Knowing that time was short, the Phantom took a quick look around. The only thing out of place was fairly obvious. On a wall covered in diplomas, licenses, testimonials and photos something was missing. From the look of the non-faded spot left on the wall whatever had been taken had been there a very long time. Reluctantly the Phantom made his way out of the house and to his car. He then drove back to Manhattan stopping only once to make an anonymous call to the police concerning the shooting.

The next day Van spent the morning putting things together. Two successful middle aged men had been murdered. The first was made to look like a suicide. The second had been murdered practically in front of him by someone the victim had either known or expected. Why had the Judge been concerned enough to have a loaded weapon handy? How were the two victims connected other than being old friends? Speaking of friends, Van looked over the list of friends of Rob Exley that Steve Huston had given him. It looked like they were mostly newspaper people; reporters and editors. Van knew or had met some of them. Before calling any of them he decided to give Steve a call.

Picking up the phone he dialed Huston's number at the *Clarion*. Steve soon picked up, "Huston, *Clarion*."

"Steve?"

Surprised but recognizing the voice Steve lowered his, "Uh, yes I'm here."

"I'm calling to see if you've found out anything more about our friend the reporter."

Steve realized that the Phantom was being circumspect and chose his words carefully, "Yes, I've located another old friend of his. Apparently they go way back and they are close now."

"Good work Steve. What's his name?

"Monsignor Frank Marchetti. He's the priest uptown at St. Katherine's. Apparently it's where Exley went to mass. He and the Monsignor have apparently been friends since college."

Van digested this for a moment, "So Father Marchetti went to Evergreen as well."

Slightly surprised Steve exclaimed, "Why yes, they both went to Evergreen State College. How did you know?"

Van smiled, "It seems everything keeps coming back to that school. Would you like to make a trip out to Connecticut with me?"

Excited, Steve didn't hesitate, "You bet, when?"

"Probably tomorrow, I'll call you at home tonight. I'll know more after I talk to the good Father." Van hung up and went into his bedroom to get dressed. Deciding that it was time to take on a new persona Van sat down at his dressing table and went to work.

By the time he was out on the street The Phantom looked totally different. His hair and complexion had been lightened a good bit. Thin rubber pieces inside his mouth filled out his cheeks and clever work with his makeup pencils changed the shape of his eyes. Clear glass lensed eyeglasses completed his new look. He was wearing a more expensive but rumpled suit. He hailed a taxi and headed up town.

Reaching St. Katherine's he paid off the cab and crossed the street to the imposing stone cathedral. He walked briskly to the rectory next door to the cathedral. Inside he inquired of a receptionist about Monsignor Marchetti. The woman was helpful and told the Phantom that the father was in the church praying. He thanked her and returned to the church. Once up the ten stone steps he pulled open one of the huge wooden doors enough to slip inside.

It was dark in the narthex and it took a moment for the Phantom's eyes to adjust. He crossed it to the rear of the lofty nave. The buttressed ceiling soared far above while rows of pews stretched forward. There was hushed silence here as the Phantom walked slowly up the aisle. He saw no one at first but as he neared the transept he made out a figure kneeling in front of the impressive apse.

The Phantom waited patiently, hat in hand. A few minutes later the black clad figure stood up, crossed himself and turned toward him. He was of moderate stature with an intelligent face. He had black hair but was going very gray. As the priest walked toward him the Phantom smiled and said, "Are you Monsignor Marchetti?"

The priest smiled and said, "I am. What can I do for you my son?"

"My name is Gray monsignor and I'd like to have a word with you if I might."

"Of course," he pointed to the first row of pews. "And it's just Father to you."

The two sat and the smiling priest spoke, "How may I help you?"

"Well Father, I was a friend of Robert Exley and I'd like to ask you a few questions."

Father Marchetti's face saddened and he crossed himself, "A terrible tragedy. Rob was such a young man. I will miss him."

The Phantom nodded, "Had you known him a long time?"

The priest got a faraway look on his face, "Yes, we went to college together. We drifted apart for some time but the last few years we've renewed our friendship." He shook his head, "I can't believe he's gone and so suddenly. But why are you asking?"

The Phantom decided that the truth or at least a good bit of it would be best, "I'm a reporter. I knew Rob and am looking into his death. They are calling it a suicide but I believe he might have been murdered." He expected the priest to be surprised if not shocked by this pronouncement but the priest listened without flinching. Nodding he looked the Phantom in the eye and spoke quietly, "I agree with you. I don't believe for an instant that Rob took his own life."

The Phantom was taken aback by the priest's honesty and certainty and asked, "Have you spoken to him recently?"

The priest nodded, "Just last week."

"Did he seem troubled?'

"Yes, I'm afraid he did."

Excited the Phantom pressed the next question, "Did he say what he was worried about?"

Father Marchetti looked sad as he spoke, "Yes, but I'm afraid I can't share anything he said."

Confused the Phantom asked, "Why Father?"

"My son everything that is spoken in the sanctuary of confession is sacred. I cannot speak of it." The Phantom was nonplussed. He hadn't even considered that Exley might have confessed to his priest. He rubbed his chin. Here were the answers he needed but there was no way the priest was going to break the sanctity of confession.

He tried decided to try a different path, "I understand. How did you come to be a priest Father?"

The cleric smiled, "My family were poor immigrants. I was born on the ship before they arrived in America. They were too poor to send me to college but I won a partial scholarship and worked my way through for the rest. I fell away from the church for a few years but after my experiences at college I came back. I graduated seminary and was ordained in 1923. My actual major in college was Political Science. That's where I met Rob."

"Did you know David Hayden or William Pearce while at college?"

The priest looked so sharply at the Phantom that for a moment he feared that the priest could see right through his disguise. The mood lightened as he nodded, "Yes, Dave and Bill and I were good friends back then as well. I haven't seen much of them the last few years although I understand that Bill has been quite successful in the legal field."

Convinced the priest knew more than he could say the Phantom chose his words carefully, "Father, I believe Rob Exley was in some kind of trouble. I also believe that someone from his past was involved in his death."

The priest smiled, "Then you suspect me?"

Speaking honestly the Phantom shook his head, "No, I don't but I believe you know more than you're saying."

"Yes I do. But as I said I am bound by vows far older than laws or conventions."

Trying for surprise the disguised detective spoke firmly, "And what if I told you that Judge Pearce was also murdered last night?"

Father Marchetti was visibly shaken. He recovered quickly. Crossing himself he said, "Poor Bill. He was a good friend. He was smart. We all knew in school that he would make a fine lawyer." He thought for a moment and looked the Phantom directly in the eye, "I still cannot speak of anything that Rob told me in confidence but I can say that if Bill Pearce was being blackmailed I know nothing about it. I have not spoken to him in over a year."

The Phantom's mind raced. Why had Father Marchetti said that? "Then Rob Exley was being blackmailed, Father?"

"I did not say that. Anything that Rob told me…"

"…is spoken in confidence," the Phantom finished his sentence. "Yes, I understand." He hesitated a moment before asking, "You aren't being blackmailed as well, are you Father?"

The priest spread his hands and smiled, "What could a blackmailer get from a poor parish priest?" He then looked innocently at the disguised detective and said, "Besides what kind of trouble could a humble priest have gotten into during his college days that would lead to blackmail."

Excited and frustrated simultaneously the Phantom was about to ask another leading question when the priest stood up suddenly. "I'm sorry but I would like to pray for Rob and Bill now if you don't mind."

The Phantom stepped back into the aisle, "Of course Father. Thank you for what you've told me . . . and especially for what you haven't."

Father Marchetti smiled as the Phantom turned to go, "I'll pray about that also." The Phantom was several steps down the aisle when the priest called to him, "Mr. Gray." The Phantom stopped and turned. The priest made the sign of the cross in the air in front of him and smiled sadly, "Go with God my son, and be careful." The Phantom nodded and strode from the church.

Once in his car and powering away from the church the Phantom decided that he was looking forward to his trip to Connecticut.

• • •

Evergreen State College was only about ninety miles away in southwestern Connecticut. In one of the Phantom's powerful cars the journey to the college campus took less than two hours. During the trip the Phantom filled in Steve on what he had found and most of what he suspected. When he had finished Steve asked, "But what could Rob and Judge Pearce be blackmailed for?"

The Phantom answered, "I don't know that they were. Father Marchetti couldn't tell me but he strongly hinted at blackmail. He also strongly hinted that it involved their college days. That's why we're going there now. Exley, Pearce, Hayden and the Father all went to college there. Something must have happened there that is at the bottom of these murders."

Steve frowned, "Then isn't Hayden likely to be in danger?"

"Perhaps. I'm going to talk to him again when I get back tonight. Hopefully we'll learn something today that will tell us what's going on.

The two sleuths reached at the college by eleven in the morning. They found a parking lot and strolled across the campus. It looked very much like what a college is supposed to look like. Wide green spaces separated dignified brick buildings. Hundreds of students streamed across the tree studded campus spilling in and out of buildings like ants. There were at least a dozen buildings and they finally had to stop a young coed and ask for directions to the administration building. Once in administration it was easy to find the registrar's office.

The registrar's office was very helpful. They easily confirmed that Exley, Pearce, Hayden and Marchetti were all graduates in the class of 1920.

All except Exley had been political science majors. He had majored in Journalism. When the Phantom casually asked if college yearbooks were kept, they were directed to the Records building. Once out on the pleasant campus Steve and the Phantom split up. The Phantom decided to visit the Political Science building to see if anyone remembered the former students. He sent Huston to the records building to look up old yearbooks that might have photos that might help. He explained to Huston, "There were old photos taken from both Exley's apartment and Pearce's house. I also believe there were books taken as well. Everything is pointing to long ago happenings here. Yearbook photos might be incriminating."

It took a few minutes to find the building housing the school of Political Science. Along the way the Phantom passed the Journalism building and marked it in his mind. It might be worth stopping there later to see if anyone remembered Exley. Once he had reached the Political Science office he inquired about long time tenured professors. The receptionist quickly directed him to Professor Arner the dean of the of the Political Science school.

After knocking and entering his office, the Phantom sized him up the professor as he came forward to shake hands. The Professor had the look of an academic. He was fairly tall and scarecrow thin. He was round shouldered and wore wire framed glasses. His hair was gray and thinning on top. Wearing his tweed suit with leather elbow patches the Phantom would have picked him out of any police line up as a college professor. He had a pleasant smile as he spoke, "Well, you're certainly not a student looking for a grade change. What can I do for you?"

"Professor Arner, they tell me you've been teaching here for over twenty years. Is that correct?"

The professor nodded as he indicated the visitor's chair in front of his desk, "Yes. I've been teaching here twenty seven years come the Fall term." He moved behind his desk and sat down, "Fine years all of them."

"Well Professor, I hope your memory is good because I'd like to ask you about some students you may have known a long time ago."

The professor smiled wryly, "That encompasses quite a few students, but go ahead I'll help you if I can."

"I'm interested in three students who graduated in 1920. All were political science majors. Their names are David Hayden, William Pearce and Frank Marchetti."

Professor Arner leaned back in his chair and thought for a moment, "I vaguely remember the Hayden boy. He was friends with the other boys.

Of course it's hard not to remember Judge Pearce. He's been back to speak on campus several times as a guest lecturer. And of course little Frankie Marchetti was very memorable." The Phantom remained outwardly calm but leaned forward slightly in anticipation, "Indeed. How so?"

"He came from a very poor family, immigrants I believe. He was a brilliant student. He won some scholarship money that allowed him to attend here but it was a struggle for him. He worked several jobs to remain in school. I myself threw some tutoring and clerical work his way to help him out."

"He was a good student you say?"

"Straight 'A's. He graduated with honors. I fully expected him to go on to graduate work. He could have had a fine career as a professor or author." He sighed, "I wonder what happened to him."

The Phantom spoke reassuringly, "I spoke to him no later than yesterday Professor. He is fine; happy and doing important work."

The professor looked surprised, "Really? What is he doing now?"

"Monsignor Marchetti is a well-respected priest in New York. But getting back to their college days, the three were friends were they?"

The professor was looking away in the distance as he spoke almost to himself, "The priesthood. Huh, I would never have thought . . . What? Oh yes, the three were good friends. The whole bunch of them were all very close."

Interested, the Phantom prompted, "Whole bunch? There were more?"

"Oh yes, there were seven or eight young men that were close friends back then."

"Can you remember any names?"

"Let's see, uh there was the Vaughan boy, his first name was Jake or Jeremy, something like that. There was also a very bright boy named Meyers. I believe he was a science major. And there a couple of others I think but I never knew their names or met all of them. I just saw the group of boys around campus."

Realizing that he was very close to something important the Phantom asked, "Do you know anything more about this group? Were they involved in any scandals? College pranks gone wrong, that sort of thing?"

"No, no. Nothing like that. They were all just good friends. I believe they had some kind informal club on campus if I recall."

The Phantom nodded, at last he was making progress, "Do you remember what kind of club it was?"

Shaking his head the professor replied, "No, I'm afraid that was all a

"Can you remember any names?"

long time ago." The Phantom stood up and held out his hand, "Thank you professor. You've been a big help. I'm impressed that you remember students that passed through your classes so long ago." The professor shrugged, "I remember all my students." The detective turned to go when the professor spoke again, "You never told me why you're asking all these questions."

The Phantom's present disguise had been prepared for just this question. "My name is Gray. I'm a reporter and I'm looking into the death of another reporter named Exley. He went to school here and I believe he was involved with your former students."

"That's too bad about your reporter friend. I wish you luck." The Phantom nodded and left the office.

Minutes later he was nearing the Records building. It was a three story brick building similar to many other campus buildings although a bit isolated. The only difference was there were no students filing in and out of it. As he neared the building bells began steadily ringing inside the building. The Phantom frowned as he started up the steps. Suddenly the front doors slammed open and people were streaming toward him. As the Phantom pushed through the frightened people, a window shattered somewhere above. Once in the small lobby he looked around but seeing no smoke sprinted for the stairway. He bounded up the steps and almost collided with a woman holding a hand over her face. As he passed he shouted, "Where's the fire?"

She coughed and gasped out, "The third floor!" and continued down the stairs. As he turned at the landing and lunged up the second half of stairs, the lights failed. The second floor was fast filling with smoke. The Phantom reached into a coat pocket, pulled out a handkerchief and clapped it over his nose and mouth. Bending forward to get below the smoke he turned to make his way to the third floor. He climbed more carefully now. Visibility was very limited. He had nearly reached the third floor when a shadowy figure loomed out of the smoke above him. With one hand on the handkerchief he could only counter one incoming punch with his free hand. The second caught him in the side of the head and sent him reeling back. He lost his footing and tumbled down four steps to the landing.

Bruised but otherwise unhurt he landed on his back. The shadowy figure attempted to hurtle across him. The Phantom threw up a leg and caught his assailant in the thigh. The shadowy figure flipped across the landing and hit the wall with a crash. The two men scrambled to their feet.

Visibility in the darkened, smoky stairwell was limited. All the Phantom could make out was a stocky man in a suit with his face covered by a white cloth up to the level of his eyes. The man stepped forward and threw a punch. The Phantom blocked and countered with a right of his own. The two exchanged several more punches in a matter of seconds. Some landed, some were blocked. Whoever he was he knew how to use his hands the Phantom thought as he blocked another punch.

The Phantom had lost his handkerchief in the fall and was forced to hold his breath while fighting. He was in superb shape thanks to regular work-outs but he could not hold his breath forever. Especially while exchanging blows at close range. Moving in the Phantom tried for a control hold but was forced to twist aside to avoid a thrusting knee. He blocked a left to his face but was caught with a sharp blow to his abdomen. Reflexively he gasped and took in some smoke. Coughing the Phantom was wide open to the stinging blow that caught him on the side of the head. Staggering back, he collided with a wall. The mysterious figure disappeared down the stairs.

Grimly the Phantom started after him and then stopped. Steve was still somewhere in this building. The fire had started on the third floor. If he was alive anywhere it was there. Getting to his hands and knees where the air was clearer he groped for his handkerchief. Holding it to his face with one hand he crawled up the stairs. It was getting very warm. By the time the Phantom made it onto the third floor he was sweating under his coat. It was even hotter here. He crawled down the dimly lit hallway calling as loudly as he could, "Steve! Steve, where are you!" The hallway was dark with smoke. He could hear the crackling of flames now and felt the furnace like heat from doorways filled with roaring flames. It was like crawling down a road to Hell.

Nearly blinded and gasping for breath between coughs, The Phantom knew he could not go much further. He nearly turned back but instead held his breath and pressed onward a little further. As he blindly reached forward along the hallway his hand touched warm flesh. It was an out stretched arm. Pressing his face close to the unconscious form he recognized the energetic reporter. A hand pressed to his throat revealed a weak pulse. Unable to stand because of the smoke the Phantom began dragging the unconscious reporter back down the hallway. Progress was slow. Starved for oxygen the Phantom grew light headed but doggedly kept up his painfully slow journey.

He had nearly reached the stairwell when he heard cracking and felt the floor beneath him shake. He rolled to his left along the floor pulling Steve with him. Across the hall a section of wall and floor collapsed. Flames spurted into the hallway. Throwing up his hand to shield his face from the heat, the Phantom grabbed Steve's collar and pulled him back down the hall away from this new threat.

The Phantom didn't have time to look for more stairs. Feeling along the wall he located a closed door across the hall from the worst of the flames. Reaching up he turned the door knob and pushed the door open. As smoke rushed into the room, the Phantom dragged the limp form into the room. He kicked the door shut and coughing looked around from the floor. File cabinets lined the walls. A small table sat in the middle of the room. Most importantly there was a window. Shakily standing he made his way across the floor. Pulling the cord he lifted the blinds all the way up and could look down on the green lawn in front of the building. Crowds of students and faculty could be seen rushing across campus and gathering a respectful distance away from the burning building. Unlocking the window he pushed the sash all the way up. Fresh air streamed into the room and the Phantom drew in a deep clean breath. Almost immediately his head cleared.

Whipping off his belt he bent over Steve's form and pulled his off as well. He linked the belts together and looped them under Steve's armpits and used it to drag Steve to the window. With the window open the room had quickly cleared of smoke. Glancing over his shoulder the Phantom could already see fresh smoke puffing under the hall door. This room too was growing uncomfortably warm. The detective leaned out of the window and looked down. Although on only the third floor, the distance down to the grass was still at least twenty feet: too far to drop Steve without chance of harm.

As soon as he had leaned out of the window dozens of people had seen him. People pointed and there were some screams. The Phantom waved and gestured. Moments later several brave souls had ran closer to the building. Cupping his hands around his mouth he shouted down, "I've got an injured man here! I need to lower him down!" There were nods and positive shouts. Ducking back the Phantom looked around. He saw nothing he could use as a rope. Frustrated for a moment he looked at the window itself and had an inspiration. He grabbed the blind's cord and yanked it loose. Doubling it he looped it through the looped belts and tied it to itself.

Gathering Steve in his arms he lifted the limp form to the window sill and swung his legs over the edge. Screams came from the growing crowd.

Holding to Steve with one hand the Shadow leaned out and shouted, "I'm going to lower him as far as I can and then you'll have to catch him." There were now at least a dozen young men gathered under the window braving the heat. As he began lowering Steve down the side of the building the Phantom marveled at people's ability to come forward and help when they were needed. Finally the Phantom was leaning as far out the window as he could and still stay braced. Steve dangled at the end of the combined belts and cord. His feet were still several feet above the heads of the crowd. They were grouped in a rough circle with some of them linking hands. The Phantom's arm ached and he was just judging the time right time to release when the overstressed cord snapped.

There was a scream from the crowd as Steve dropped straight into the arms of the waiting crowd. They easily caught his weight and lowered him safely to the ground. The Phantom drew in a long breath and glanced over his shoulder. The door to the room was smoldering and small tongues of flame were licking under it. It was time to go. He swung his leg over the sill and carefully lowered himself to the length of his arms. He hung there a moment as windows shattered above and around him. He could hear sirens growing louder. Carefully the Phantom moved his right hand down the face of the wall attempting to find finger holds between the cemented bricks. He found one and lowered a leg scrabbling for a toe hold. He repeated this effort with his left hand and gained a few feet of safety. Concentrating, he blocked out the shouts, screams and now deafening sirens. He gained another foot and looked up. Smoke was now pouring out of the open window he had just left. His attention diverted, the Phantom lost his grip and fell outward.

Not wanting to cartwheel down the Phantom pushed off the wall with his feet and dropped straight down. His legs flexed to take impact he landed hard, turning an ankle slightly as he collapsed back against a would-be rescuer who had rushed forward to help break his fall. The bystander helped him to his feet and they both fled away from the burning building.

Once among the crowd solicitous people led him further away. Fire trucks were pulling up at the building and firemen were laying out hose. Further away an ambulance stood by. One of the attendants leaned over Steve giving him oxygen from a portable tank. Other people with minor injuries were receiving first aid. The Phantom looked back at the stately brick building. Smoke was pouring out of every window. The building would probably be a total loss. The Phantom turned away to make sure Steve received proper treatment. He soon revived enough to give the

Phantom a weak smile as he was be bundled into the ambulance. Slipping away through the growing crowd the Phantom eventually reached his car and powered away after it.

The local hospital was not a large one but thankfully had not been overwhelmed by the few fire casualties. The burned building had not been heavily occupied and injuries were few; mostly smoke inhalation and minor burns. It turned out that Steve was the most seriously injured person treated. While he waited for news a solicitous doctor looked at his rather scorched hands. The doctor treated and bandaged up the few blisters, checked his heart and breath and pronounced him sound. The Phantom could not say the same for his battered suit; it was scorched and torn.

Eventually he was admitted to Steve's room. He had spoken to the doctor and Steve had a concussion from a blow to the back of his head, minor burns on hands and legs but would recover with no permanent damage. In fact he probably would be released tomorrow. When they finally had a moment alone the Phantom pasted a positive smile on his face and said, "The doctor says you're going to make it Steve."

Steve smiled weakly, "Thanks to you. I don't remember getting out at all. How did you do it?"

The Phantom waved a dismissive hand, "I had help from some brave folks on the scene. You don't remember anything at all about what happened?"

"Not about getting out but I remember plenty about finding the book."

"Book? You found something?"

"Boy did I! I was directed to a large room with shelves of books and school records. There was a whole shelf of school yearbooks going back a long way. I concentrated on the years 1916-1920. In the 1919 year book there was a small picture of some boys gathered in front of one of the campus buildings. They were all young and smiling. I immediately recognized Rob Exley. Excited, I moved over to the window for better light and bamm! The lights went out. I woke up with my head feeling like it split in two."

"How long were you out?"

"Couldn't have been too long otherwise I'd be a cooked goose. The room was on fire but it hadn't spread too far." The Phantom nodded for him to continue, "Any way I made for the door but I was trapped. The only way was through the flames so I took a run and dove over them through the door way. I rolled into the hall but I'm afraid a got my tail feathers scorched. He indicated his bandaged legs with one similarly bandaged hand."

The Phantom grimaced in sympathy. Steve shrugged, "The hallway was already filling with smoke and the alarm had gone off. I got down on my knees and tried to find the stairs. I don't know how far I got before I finally passed out. Where did you find me?"

"Not far from the stairwell. You almost made it. It was nip and tuck there for a minute but I found us an exit."

Steve looked around furtively and lowered his voice, "Thanks Phantom. If it wasn't for you I'd . . ." He trailed off as the Phantom smiled, "All that counts is you made it out. But you didn't get a look at whoever hit you?"

Steve carefully rubbed the back of his head, "No. He got me from behind."

The detective shook his head sadly, "It's too bad about the book. I think it's an important clue to what's going on."

Steve smiled widely, "I wouldn't worry about the book. It probably came through better than I did."

The Phantom looked quizzical. Steve continued, "When I woke up the room was burning, like I said. I opened the window and saw there was no fire escape. I knew I would have to make a dash for it and there was no way I could carry the book so. . ." He paused for dramatic effect, "I threw it out the window before I took off. It's probably lying in the grass right now."

Leaning forward the detective patted Steve gently on the shoulder, "Quick thinking Steve. I'll go and find it right now. Rest here and I'll take you back to the city tomorrow."

After getting precise directions about the book's location the Phantom immediately drove back to the college. The fire had been extinguished and the crowd had dwindled significantly. Unfortunately there were still firefighters and police everywhere. Realizing that his appearance would make him a target of questions the disguised sleuth slipped back to his car and waited.

By sunset things had quieted down. The firemen had rolled up their hoses and gone home as had the police. The building was roped off and posted with signs but the Phantom could get fairly close to it. Using his flashlight he went to the area where Steve indicated the book had landed. It took some time to find it, There was quite a lot of debris scatted across the grass and the water soaked grass had been trampled and torn up by the fire-fighting efforts. He finally found it about twenty feet from the building. Examining it by flashlight he could see the book was the worse for wear. It was not scorched but it had considerable water damage. Fire hoses and lying in the wet grass for hours had not done it any good. Handling it carefully the Phantom headed for his car. Driving into town he located the closest hotel to the hospital and booked a room for the night.

The next morning the Phantom picked Steve up at the hospital. The two had not gone far when the Phantom pulled over the car and got out the yearbook. Steve quickly located the photo he had found. The book had dried somewhat but the page was still wrinkled and the image was hard to make out. It showed eight young smiling men photographed in front of one of the campus buildings. The caption underneath was unreadable. The Phantom pointed to the men, "I can make out Exley, Pearce, Hayden and Father Marchetti but I don't recognize any of the others do you?"

Steve nodded affirmatively, "I recognize the stocky fellow there. He used to be a police detective some years back. I can't remember his name, Jack something, I think he was fired from the force. And I know this fellow." He touched the image of a tall, thin youth, "This is Jason Vaughan. He's an ex-assistant District Attorney. He quit the DA's office awhile back. He's still lawyering but recently he announced that he's running for city council this fall."

The Phantom nodded. He recognized the name, having read of Vaughan in the newspapers. The two sleuths both agreed that neither recognized the last two men. Closing the book they resumed their trip back to the city.

Two hours later the Phantom pulled his car over in front of the residence of Frank Havens. Steve was surprised to learn that the Phantom had arranged for Steve to stay with Havens for a few days while he recovered. Before he continued on his way, Steve promised him he would do what research he could on Vaughan and the ex-policeman while he rested with the *Clarion's* editor.

Back at his apartment Van stripped out of his disguise and cleaned up. When he had eaten he retired to his hidden sanctum to do some research. He carefully dried the page of the yearbook that interested him. He then used a reagent to bring up the faded caption. That helped but he finally needed an ultra violet lamp to allow him to read it. The caption read *Circle of Hope* a political club. Satisfied, Van decided that after a good night's sleep he would make another call on Father Marchetti, after he had made another visit.

The next morning found the Phantom entering the office building of attorney Vaughan. He was again disguised as a newspaper reporter. Locating the attorney's office he was just entering the office as a tall well-dressed man with a briefcase was leaving. He spoke, "Are you Jason Vaughan?"

The handsome man gave the Phantom a prepackaged smile, "I am."

The Phantom stuck out his hand, "My name is Gray. I'm with the *Clarion*. I wonder if I might have a minute of your time."

The lawyer locked his door and looked at his watch, "I'm afraid I'm late for an appointment. However you can walk out with me."

Nodding his assent the Phantom followed him to the elevator. Opening his notebook he then asked, "About your campaign. How is it being financed?"

The candidate looked sharply at him, "All of my contributions are from individuals. I'm taking no money from big business or labor unions. You'll find no corruption in my campaign."

Nodding the Phantom scribbled in his book, "I'm doing my article from a 'man of the people' point of view. I've spoken with your old professors at Evergreen and they speak highly of you. You also got a glowing endorsement from my parish priest." That merited another sharp look from the lawyer.

The elevator doors opened and the two strode across the lobby. As they did the Phantom questioned, "Do you have any comment on the death of Judge Pearce?"

Vaughan stopped just short of the front doors and looked sharply once more at his interrogator, "Bill Pearce was one of my oldest friends. His death is a blow to this city and a personal tragedy for me. I hope they find his killer and prosecute him to the fullest extent of the law."

Scribbling furiously in his notebook the Phantom nodded, "A fine quote Mr. Vaughan." Before he could ask anything else the lawyer pushed through the front doors. The doorman was waving a cab over and Vaughan was reaching for the door. He looked back, "I'm sorry I don't have any more time. Call my office and we'll talk again." He entered the taxi and it pulled away. The Phantom closed his notebook and looked thoughtfully after the departing lawyer. The Phantom made his way back to his car and drove uptown.

Having called ahead, the disguised Phantom once more pulled his car to a stop near St. Katherine's church. This time the Father was waiting for him in a rear row of pews. After shaking hands they walked forward, nearing the apse the Father crossed himself and sat. The Phantom turned to him and spoke, "I'm sorry to bother you again Father but I have a few more questions."

Father Marchetti smiled, "Of course."

The Phantom told the priest of his trip to the school. He told of his discovery of the photograph and the men they had identified then asked, "Who are the other men of your group."

The priest looked at the Phantom's bandaged hands and frowned. He then spoke in a calm voice, "Irwin Meyers was one. He's a successful physician now. Also there was Matthew Shrum. He went into banking here in the city. Finally I believe the man your friend identified is Jack Taggart. I heard that he had left the police force. I don't know why but he was always a wild one."

The Phantom nodded thoughtfully, "Father I think someone, possibly one of your friends is responsible for the deaths of Exley and Pearce and I believe you know something about it."

The reverend crossed himself, "I am sorry about Rob and Bill but I don't know who killed them. I do know that Rob was afraid. I believe he came to not only confess but to warn me. If one of my old friends is responsible for all this then I am saddened. I will pray for their souls."

Knowing that he would not get any more from the man about Rob's confession the Phantom stood up. The priest walked with him back toward the church doors. As they neared the doors the Phantom asked, "Your group, it was a political group wasn't it?"

Father Marchetti smiled, "We were all so young and enthusiastic. We thought we could change the world. Perhaps the world wasn't ready."

"Was your group radical?"

The priest shook his head, "Who's to say what is radical and what is just different? I'm just a priest not a philosopher."

The cleric pulled open one of the large doors and followed the Phantom out onto the stone steps. They were shaking hands when over the priest's shoulder he saw a man across the street at the mouth of an alley aiming a weapon. The Phantom lunged forward knocking the Father Marchetti to the concrete. A shot rang out. The bullet whistled overhead and ricocheted off the marble façade of the church above their heads.

In a flash the Phantom was up and reaching for his gun. Instead of exchanging gunfire the stocky figure turned and disappeared down the alley. Steadying his gun in his bandaged hands the Phantom took aim but had no shot. Holding his fire he instead leaped down the steps in pursuit.

Sprinting across the street the Phantom flattened himself against the wall next to the alley and carefully looked around the corner. It was empty. His pistol leading, he crept carefully down the alley. It ended at a wider alley running at right angles behind the row of buildings. It was also empty save for the usual collection of discarded items and overflowing garbage cans. He heard a car start at the end of the block and sprinted that way. Too late all he could see when he reached the side street was a dark colored sedan disappearing down the street.

"The bullet whistled overhead…"

Back at the church he found the Father shaken but unharmed. In the rectory they had a short conversation before he left. The Phantom decided to tackle Shrum, Meyers and Taggart the next day. Once home he called Havens to report and then retired for the night.

The next day the Phantom called on Matthew Shrum. He was admitted readily to the vice president of the United Commerce Bank's office. He stated his purpose but at the name Robert Exley the bank executive suddenly had an attack of amnesia. He stared hard at the Phantom and spoke carefully; "Rob Exley and Bill Pearce were two of my closest friends in college. Unfortunately I have not seen much of either of them the last few years. I'm afraid I know nothing about their deaths. Tragic as they were." His answers to additional questions were just as unhelpful. Thanking him the Phantom left his office.

Deciding to try something different with Dr. Shrum the Phantom called and arranged an appointment for later that day giving his name as Johnson. He then stopped for lunch to kill time.

Later he took a taxi to Dr. Meyers' office. He was quickly admitted to the doctor's office. As they shook hands he studied the doctor. He was stocky, dark haired and of course approximately forty years of age, the same as the rest of the Circle. When settled in a chair the doctor inquired, "What can I do for you Mr. Johnson?"

Going for shock the Phantom looked steadily at the doctor, "Actually my name is Gray and I'm looking into the deaths of Judge Pearce and Robert Exley. I know you and they and five others belonged to a Group called the *Circle of Hope* in college. I believe that one of your group is responsible for those deaths. Care to comment?"

The moment the Phantom had begun speaking the doctor's mouth had dropped open. Then it had closed and his expression had gone dead. His complexion paled whether in anger or fear the detective could not tell. He stood and in a whisper said, "You'd better go! Now!"

The Phantom rose and smiled menacingly at the Dr. Meyers, "This isn't going away doctor and neither am I." He left the white coated doctor sitting there looking shocked.

Satisfied that he had properly rattled enough cages, the Phantom caught a taxi to the Green Spot. He ordered a beer and while he waited he called the home of the *Clarion's* editor. He recognized Steve Huston's voice and identified himself as Mr. Gray. Recognizing the Phantom's alias Steve greeted him enthusiastically. After inquiring about Steve's health and being reassured that he was on the mend, the two got down to business.

Steve was enthused, "I've been doing some calling around. I found out that Jack Taggart was a detective on the police force. He was suspended from the force nearly two years ago for excessive use of force against a suspect. He tried to get reinstated but no soap. He even got letters of recommendation from Judge Pearce and then assistant DA Vaughan." The Phantom then asked if he had an address for Taggart. Steve's answer was disappointing, "I'm having trouble getting a line on that. He moved with no forwarding address a few weeks ago. No one seems to know where he is. I've got a hunch he's lying low. You don't think he's behind this do you?"

The Phantom answered non-committedly, "I don't know what to think Steve. Anything on the others?"

"Well, the word I get is that Judge Pearce was on Vaughan's election campaign committee. He even ran a fund raiser for him a couple of months back. I'm trying to get the invitation list but it may take a while."

"That's fine work from a sick bed Steve."

"I'm not in bed just taking it easy and working the phones. Oh the word around is that Vaughan stands a good chance to win the election if he runs a good campaign. The incumbent is fighting charges of corruption but he has deep pockets."

"You've given me a lot to think about. Thanks." The Phantom hung up and went back to his beer. As he sipped he thought about what he knew. Exley had been killed but it had been made to look like a suicide, why? To cover up something certainly, but what? But why had Pearce been killed? What had he been writing that night when the Phantom saw him? Father Marchetti had hinted strongly about blackmail. But who was blackmailing who? It was obvious now that the photos and books taken from the two dead men had related to the college group of friends. Who but one of the original Circle would want to hide a connection to the dead men? It all came back the Circle.

That night Van decided to take a closer look at the private homes of some of the Circle. He again chose his rumpled reporter look. It was average enough not to attract attention but decent enough to appear above suspicion. Once disguised and equipped he picked up one his cars and drove north. Dr. Meyers lived in a pricey brownstone on the Upper East Side. He wanted to get in and look around when no one was there. Driving past he saw lights on in the house and drove past.

He then headed north to his next target. Shrum the banker lived in a nice house in the Bronx. It was a large house with a small yard. Parking around the corner the Phantom strolled casually past the house. It was in total darkness. Reaching the corner he crossed the street and walked back down the street. All was peaceful. Most houses showed lights but the street was empty. When he was opposite Shrum's house again he crossed the street. He was in the middle of the street when something caught his eye. It was movement of some sort down the street. The Phantom continued across the small front yard of the banker's house and ducked behind the corner of it. He leaned around just enough to watch the darkened street.

A moment later he heard a car door open and saw shadowy movement near a dark colored coupe parked down the block. He watched but the figure disappeared under the shadow of a low hanging tree. The Phantom frowned and faded down the side of the house. Reaching a fence he quickly scrambled over it into the small back yard. It would be foolish to break into the house now when he was being watched. He briefly considered drawing his gun and waiting for the hidden watcher but quickly discarded this idea. Whoever these men were they weren't afraid of burning buildings or killing to protect their secrets. Starting a gun fight in this neighborhood of homes would be irresponsible.

He continued around the house past a detached garage and passed through an open gate. As he did he thought he could hear wood scraping on the other side of the house. The watcher was following him. Quickly the Phantom sprinted to the sidewalk and down to his car. Throwing himself behind the wheel he fired up the powerful engine and screeched away. He left his headlights off for several blocks and made a few turns. Once he was sure that there was no pursuit he considered. Whoever it was had been waiting for him. How many enemies were out there?

Quickly he put the wheel over and drove back into the city. A half hour later he parked on an Upper West Side street and walked to a high rise apartment building. He kept a close look out but saw no one taking an interest in him. In the lobby of the apartment building he approached the doorman and showed his detective badge. The smile fell off the doorman's face as the Phantom said, "Detective Gray. I'm undercover and here to check on a suspect."

The doorman queried, "Who do you want to see sir?"

Shaking his head the Phantom told him, "That's classified. Also you are not to mention that anyone from the police was here to any of your tenants. Is that clear?"

The doorman nodded his understanding. The Phantom moved quickly to the door marked *Stairs* and disappeared. He climbed briskly to Jason Vaughan's floor and had a story ready as he knocked on the door. There was no answer so he knocked again. As he hoped the Attorney was out. Using his master key he had the door open in seconds.

Once in the apartment he moved quickly. Ignoring the well-furnished living room he moved to the bedrooms. As he suspected one of them was being used as an office. He ignored the expensively decorated bedroom and went for the office.

Inside he was immediately attracted to the wall of framed photos. There were the usual degrees and licenses but also many large photos. There were images of the attorney with family and with city and state officials. Most interesting were several photos of him with friends. The Phantom immediately recognized several with Pearce and Taggart. Suddenly there it was sandwiched between his law degree and a photo of he and the former mayor; an old photo of eight young men wearing casual clothing all standing in front of a foreign flag. It was the *Circle of Hope*. This or a similar photo was undoubtedly what had been missing from Exley's and Pearce's walls. Seeing it explained everything. The Phantom now understood what it was all about. He turned to go but instead went through the attorney's desk. Sorting through Vaughan's personal papers proved quite interesting.

Turning off lights as he went the Phantom quickly let himself out of the apartment. Once in the lobby he nodded conspiratorially at the doorman as he exited onto the street. He watched carefully as he made his way to his car but saw no one following him. Once in it he drove back to Park Avenue.

In his apartment he stripped off his disguise and settled down with a drink. He considered the situation for a few minutes before he decided on a course of action. Picking up the phone he dialed the office of Frank Havens. Havens was working late as he often did and the Phantom was quickly connected. He identified himself as Gray when Havens answered and said, "Frank, I know why Rob Exley was killed."

"That's great news. What's behind it all?"

"I can't tell you over the phone but I promise I'll explain everything soon. Right now I need a favor."

"Certainly."

"Good there's a little meeting I want you to organize. Here are the particulars . . . "

● ● ●

Two evenings later the editor of the *Clarion* entered the exclusive Publisher's Club. Checking his hat and coat he moved through the club greeting several friends and associates as he made his way to a private meeting room. Waiting for him just outside the door was a dignified figure dressed in black. Holding out his hand Havens spoke, "You must be Monsignor Marchetti." The priest smiled back, "It's just Father, Mr. Havens. Thank you for inviting me."

"Not at all, Father. Come in."

The meeting room had series of chairs set in a large circle. There was table set up with food and drink to one side. There was also a connecting door in a side wall. Soon the door opened and the thin, studious figure of Dave Hayden entered. He immediately recognized Father Marchetti and there was some joyous hand pumping and back slapping. The two friends were soon joined by Dr. Meyers and the banker Shrum. Havens had been supplied with names and descriptions and greeted each man as he arrived and thanked him for coming to the 'fund raiser.' Both newcomers were just as surprised to see their old friends as Hayden had been.

Last to join the gathering was the former detective Taggart. The stocky former cop seemed the most surprised of all when he entered, though he was greeted by his old school friends as enthusiastically as the others. Havens looked at his watch. It was just seven fifteen. He excused himself and left the room. He walked quickly to the manager's office and returned a few minutes later. Instead of re-entering the meeting, he instead moved to the main entry.

He had only a few minutes to wait. Soon a tall, well-dressed man entered. As he was removing his hat and overcoat, Havens stepped forward. He offered his hand to the attorney Jason Vaughan and led him back to the meeting room. When Vaughan entered there was even more acclaim as his friends surrounded him. He was totally surprised as he shook hands with his old friends.

Eventually Havens was able to get the attention of the men and direct them to chairs. When they were all seated he spoke, "Thank you all for coming to this gathering for Mr. Vaughan. I'm sure you all know that he is running for city council and needs as much support as he can get. As some of his oldest friends I thought it appropriate that you all come together tonight in his honor." At these words the side door opened and a tall, well-built man entered.

He wore a dark suit and fedora. He was olive skinned and his features were obscured by a black domino mask. As he stepped through the door everyone turned to look at the new figure. There were startled exclamations and intakes of breath. Taggart the former detective exclaimed, "The Phantom!" and reached for his coat. In an instant an automatic pistol appeared in the Phantom's hand pointed straight at Taggart's face. He spoke in a calm voice, "I don't want to shoot you but you've tried to kill me at least twice in the last few days and I'm not too worried about whether you make it to jail safely." Taggart's hand froze halfway inside of his coat. Then he slowly removed it holding a revolver that he carefully dropped to the floor. The Phantom nodded.

Stepping forward he spoke in a firm voice, "Mr. Havens, welcome to the first organized meeting of the *Circle of Hope* in twenty years." At these words there were gasps, shocked looks and open mouths. The only exception was the placid face of Father Marchetti. Speaking to Havens but keeping his eyes on Taggart, the Phantom continued, "These men, along with William Pearce and Robert Exley went to college together at Evergreen State College. There they formed a political club; the 'Circle.'

The Phantom went on to tell Havens that although of various backgrounds their socialist leanings had brought them together as friends. Fascinated by the writings of Marx and inspired by the Russian revolution of 1917 they formed their club with the intention of becoming a branch of the then brand new American Communist Party. From this same inspiration came a wave of radical violence that swept the country. The government grew concerned and using the Sedition Act of 1918 began breaking up Communist groups and arresting members of the party. He paused and Havens asked, "And the Circle?"

Keeping his gun steady the Phantom waved his free hand at the group of men. "They disbanded their group and drifted apart after graduation. They then went on to become lawyers, doctors, and priests, solid citizens all." He went on to say that no one had ever spoken of their past. They had all gone to their chosen careers with no one aware of their past. The only exception had been Father Marchetti who regretting his political affiliations had entered the seminary with the intention of helping mankind in a different way. During this monologue the group members had different reactions. There were looks of surprise, embarrassment even anger.

Havens looked thoughtfully at the group, "That explains their connection but why were Rob Exley and Judge Pearce killed."

The Phantom frowned, "Someone found out about their past. That someone began blackmailing some of the group, probably the wealthier members." Both Shrum and Meyers looked uncomfortable. The Phantom continued, "It wouldn't have done much good blackmailing the good father, Mr. Hayden or Rob Exley. They just didn't have enough money to be worth blackmailing. I believe that somehow Exley found out about the blackmail and figured out who was behind it. For that he was killed and the death made to look like a suicide."

The masked figure continued, "After Exley's death, Judge Pearce decided not to pay any more blackmail. I saw him write out what I believe were details of the blackmail scheme. Unfortunately that document was stolen by whoever shot him." He spoke to Taggart, "That was the first time you tried to kill me, the night you murdered the Judge. You got away with the letter he wrote plus evidence of the Circle."

Taggart licked his lips and gritted out, "You don't have any proof!" Simultaneously there were gasps and exclamations from the rest of the group. Ignoring him the Phantom continued, "You also nearly killed me at Evergreen along with Steve Huston the *Clarion* reporter. We fought in the stairwell. It was too dark to identify you but it could be no one else. As for proof, I believe the police will be able to match your gun to bullets recovered at the Judge's house." Taggart looked grim. The Phantom continued, "I wasn't sure why you were involved until I looked into your background. The truth is you were just doing the real blackmailer's dirty work."

At this the Phantom was greeted with a hushed silence and rapt looks of attention. He swung his pistol and lined it up on Jason Vaughan, "Wasn't he Counselor?" There were more gasps among the former friends. Looking cool the attorney replied, "That's ridiculous. You have no evidence for these accusations. I'll sue you for defamation of character." The Phantom laughed, "You're the only wealthy member of the Circle that wasn't being blackmailed. Plus you badly needed money to fund your campaign. I think that when the police start looking into your finances they'll find no mysterious withdrawals to pay blackmail money but lots of questionable cash deposits. I'm sure they'll also find out that you've been paying Taggart to do your dirty work. I'd wager that you've promised to have him reinstated on the force after you're elected haven't you?" At these words both Vaughan and Taggart looked nervous. The masked figure had one last accusation, "I'm sure Taggart killed Pearce and set the fire at Evergreen. He was probably the one who tried to kill Father Marchetti also. But I have strong suspicion that it was you who murdered Rob Exley Counselor." Taggart tried to laugh nervously while Vaughan visibly paled.

The Phantom could see angry and shocked looks on the faces of the rest of the group. He nodded at Havens who moved to the door. Havens opened it and waved a hand. In stepped Inspector Gregg with handcuffs in his hand. He was followed by three uniformed officers. Close behind, Steve Huston slipped into the room his notepad in his bandaged hands.

As the inspector jerked Taggart to his feet he said, "Good work Phantom. We'll take it from here."

The Phantom stowed away his pistol beneath his jacket. As he quietly slipped out the side door he saw Vaughan and Taggart being led away as Havens and Huston began questioning the Circle members for details.

● ● ●

Three days later Dick Van Loan was being shown to a table in the fashionable Poltroons Club. As usual Havens was early and waiting for him. He greeted the editor, sat down and was handed a menu. As he was perusing it he remarked, "Well, it looks like the *Clarion* has another scoop. Good article by Steve Huston." He smiled, "Blackmail and murder certainly make for good headlines."

The editor smiled in return, "They certainly do, especially when they involve prominent citizens and political candidates. But now it's time to give up all those details I haven't heard yet."

Van nodded, "I knew Exley and the Judge were almost certainly killed by someone they knew, someone who was trying to hide evidence from the past. It had to be someone from their college group. I didn't find out all the members of the group until Steve located the yearbook photo at the college. That helped but I finally figured it all out when I saw the photo on Vaughan's office wall. It showed the entire group of friends gathered in front of a Red Communist flag. That finally confirmed that it all revolved around blackmail. Then it was just a matter of deduction. Who had the most to lose and gain? Marchetti was not a suspect, in fact he tried to give me what information he could. Pearce, Shrum, Meyers and Vaughan were the wealthier members of the group. Vaughan was one who needed money the most and was also the only one who didn't seem nervous at being questioned."

"And Taggart?"

"The figure at Pearce's house, the college and St. Katherine's was too strong and stocky to be Vaughan. Only Taggart fit the bill. He and Vaughan also had a long history when Vaughan was an assistant DA. I'm glad you managed to locate him in time for our little gathering."

Havens smiled, "It took some work but I had Inspector Gregg to help." He then spoke more humbly, "Thanks Van. This case was personal for me and I appreciate everything you've done."

Van smiled in return, "Every case is personal to someone. The next one will be as well." He waved the waiter over to order lunch.

THE END

Secrets of the Circle

How did I come to write a *Phantom Detective* Story? The proper question might why did it take so long for me to write a *PD* story? I mean, who wouldn't want to write a story about one of the longest lived pulp heroes? *The Phantom Detective* ran for twenty years, longer than *The Shadow*. Plus, literally dozens of pulp authors wrote stories about him. So why would I not want to join those storied ranks? The answer: of course I would.

The Phantom wasn't necessarily my favorite hero; I tend to favor the mysterious masked avengers who slip through the night terrorizing the underworld with blazing automatics. It must be noted, that in his early books the Phantom did some of that kind of thing as well, although not as much later in the series. Still, the Phantom Detective was high on my list of pulp heroes to write about so I kept an eye out for opportunities. Airship 27 had never done a Phantom Detective book but I figured it was just a matter of time and I had developed a good idea ready for a fast draw when needed. So when Ron Fortier put out a call for stories I was all over it.

As I said I had a good story idea ready when the time came. The Phantom Detective ran for a long time and went through a lot of changes. I chose my story to match the style of the later stories. No bizarre plots and colorful villains but more of a pure detective story. I wanted something with a series of victims, lots of clues and a mystery villain. So I went to my library and started sorting through the old pulps. Walter Gibson as well as other pulp authors used to be very good at this sort of thing and sure enough I found several good stories to inspire me. In the end I decided to go with some classic themes: suicide, blackmail and murder. How can that not make for a good story?

The actual writing of the story went smooth and quickly. So quickly, that I broke my daily word record one day. I pretty much wrote the whole thing in six days. It needed tightening as all stories do but not a lot. In the end I think it is a pretty good story.

I felt comfortable with the Phantom. He is more of a pure detective than an actual masked avenger but he was still a lot of fun to write about and it never hurts to get some mystery writing experience. Mysteries are, after all a literary staple. The hardest thing about writing mysteries is keeping, all the victims, clues, villains straight. Timing is important also.

Sometimes writing a mystery is almost a juggling act, trying to keep all the clues and suspects in the air at once.

The historical premise I used for the background of the victims is accurate. There was a "Red" scare in this country not long after the Russian October revolution. The overthrow of one of the world's longest monarchies had given credibility to Marxism and new life to socialist and communist movements. After a burst of violence here in America, eventually laid mainly at the feet of anarchists, the U.S. Government led a crackdown on communists in this country using the Sedition Act of 1918 as a justification. Many were arrested or deported. It lasted several years and drove many communist sympathizers underground. This seemed like a good skeleton for my characters to have in their closets.

I hope you enjoy the Phantom Detective's adventures in *Circle of Despair*. This will be *Airship 27's* first book of what I hope are many Phantom Detective volumes. I am excited to be part of it and pleased that I have joined the ranks of writers such as Norman Daniels, Charles Greenburg and dozens of others who have chronicled the adventures of The Phantom Detective. Maybe I'll see you again in future volumes.

• • •

GENE MOYERS—studied European and Medieval history at the University of Oregon. He is a former U.S. Army armor crewman. He worked in the High Tech industry for some time and ran a store front and internet hobby shop for several years. An avid military gamer and role player his favorite game was *Daredevils* set in the 1930s. His love affair with the 1930s and pulps in particular stem from his first time reading a *Shadow* novel as a boy. Although interested in writing since a teen he did not turn to serious writing until 2000. He is the co-author of *GURPS Crusades* published by Steve Jackson Games. He has a story published in *Ravenwood* volume II by Airship 27. He has also written stories that will appear in the future volumes of *Moon Man* and *The Purple Scar*. When not working on Airship 27 projects he is busy writing horror adventures for his swashbuckling character set in Colonial America.

Gene currently lives in Beaverton Oregon with his wife and three lazy dogs.

Campaign of Destruction

by Whit Howland

S everal patrons crouched in terror on the marble floor of State Bank
and Trust. A hoodlum lorded over the frightened throng as he stood
on the counter. He waved his Tommy gun like a metronome.

Cloaking his face was a pillowcase with eyeholes. He also wore a black
duster. Pinned to his lapel was a chrome diamond-studded skull, brand-
ing him the dastardly gangster, Stickpin.

Stickpin's compatriots dressed in similar garb. They worked feverishly,
pillaging the cash in the teller drawers. As they stuffed the dough in burlap bags, the ring leader looked at the large wall clock. The minute hand's
nervous tick caused a wave of adrenaline to roll through his veins.

"Get to the vault!"

The order made the three other holdup men take pause.

"You heard me, get to the vault!"

"But, boss, we ain't gotta 'nuff time, the bulls'll be here any second," the
thug closest to him replied.

Stickpin leveled his heater at the man. "Get to the vault or you'll be
pushin' up daisies!"

The cutthroat scurried across the floor, jumped over a large oak desk,
and disappeared from sight. When he emerged, he dragged a bald, be-
spectacled man in a shirt and tie by the suspenders. He hustled him to
the vault. Buckets of sweat dripped from the bank manager's forehead as
he worked the combination. Every now and then the gunman gave him a
hard nudge to hurry him along.

"Come on, speed it up or I'll snuff your pilot light!" the robber snarled.

The little man coughed and shook as he tried to open the safe. His captor pressed the barrel of his weapon to the side of the supervisor's head.
He racked the shotgun. The man, drenched in perspiration, looked plead-
ingly at the desperado. The thug flipped the gun around and smacked him
across the face with the walnut stock.

The robber then turned to his leader. "Boss, we gotta go. The coppers
are on the way for sure!"

Stickpin glowered through the slits in the cloth at his henchman. The
other burglar felt the daggers pierce his soul. When he turned around, he

72

found the bald man gone. Before he had time to react, his world turned fuzzy, then black, as his knees buckled and he fell to the floor.

Standing over him was a tall wraith in a gray trench coat. A diamond-shaped badge stuck to his chest. To hide his facial features, the figure wore a fedora and donned a domino mask. He was the Phantom Detective.

With the utmost stealth, the Phantom Detective crept along the floor hiding behind desks and counters. Sneaking up on one of Stickpin's confederates, he grabbed him by the neck, snapped it, and gently guided the lifeless form to the ground. A panicked customer foiled his intended silent killing spree as she let out a loud gasp. The vigilante tried to *shush* the frightened damsel. But it was too late!

The commotion caught the attention of Stickpin causing him to emit a guttural cry. Squeezing the trigger, he unleashed lead-filled fury. The customers screamed. The Phantom Detective ducked behind a counter. Pieces of granite skittered across the floor.

The crime fighter retorted with two wild shots and then dove for the big desk. The other brutes' machine guns rattled away, splintering the oak that buffered the Phantom Detective. When the opportunity arose, the Phantom flipped upright onto the top of the desk, drew his chrome forty-fives, and faced the hatchet man at the far end of the teller's counter. With both belching barrels, he plugged his adversary.

Causing a tornado of papers, he spun off the desk. In midair he ended another goon's life with a single shot to the heart. Rolling on the ground, he dodged more of Stickpin's fire before diving behind a counter. Stickpin disappeared behind another counter and popped back up holding a terrified employee in a headlock. The muzzle of his gun jammed into the skinny man's ear.

"Drop 'em or I decorate the place with his brains!" Stickpin sneered.

The Phantom Detective rose slowly from his breastwork, training his pistols at the gangster.

"I said drop 'em or the working stiff's a dead man!"

"Go ahead, shoot him," the Phantom calmly replied.

Stickpin jerked his head back in surprise. The Phantom fired two shots. One hit the back wall and the other landed squarely in Stickpin's gut. He released his hostage as he crumpled to the marble floor.

The crusader swooped down on the hoodlum like a war bird. He breathed fiery breath in Stickpin's face as he readied himself to finish off his prey. The malcontent shuddered.

"Don't kill me! Please don't kill me!" Stickpin pleaded.

"So long, creep!" the Phantom Detective replied as he cooled his opponent. A death twitch marked the end of Stickpin's turbulent and bloody life.

Blaring police sirens kept the hero from admiring his handy work. As they grew louder, he raced for the door and was gone.

He exited the bank just as two patrol cars pulled up to the entrance.

"Halt, Phantom!" a cop yelled.

The Phantom accelerated and turned into an alley. The passage was long and narrow and the exit seemed miles away. As he was running, a policeman stepped out in front of him and attempted to clothesline the vigilante with his nightstick. The Phantom Detective dodged his assailant but collided with the wall.

The cop drew his weapon. "Hands up!"

"Can't do it!" With a roundhouse, the Phantom kicked the gun from the flatfoot's hand. The officer jumped out of the way. The Phantom Detective spun behind the policeman. The centurion started to turn but he wasn't fast enough.

The crime fighter put him in a chokehold and rendered him unconscious. The Phantom broke the man's fall. He didn't want to hurt the gent with the badge since they were on the same side, so he lowered him to the asphalt. With the policeman incapacitated, the hero continued on his journey.

• • •

Police sirens screamed as the clandestine guardian finessed the wheel of his flaming red sportster. Their cars proved deceptively fast and nipped at the tail of the sleek machine. The vanquisher weaved in and out of traffic. He skidded and made hard turns onto side streets. One police vehicle brushed up on his bumper as the Phantom made his way to a large thoroughfare.

His hot rod headed straight for two other patrol cars in a perilous game of chicken. It was the men in uniform who blinked as one veered right and the other left. They passed the avenger, turned and continued pursuit.

The black and whites then clung like leeches to the Phantom Detective. It was time for counter measures. The masked man pressed a button on his dashboard full of dials, gauges, knobs, and levers.

Tiny hoses popped out of the vehicle's shiny fender and squirted oil onto the street. The slick caused the cruisers to spin out of control; just the advantage the hero needed. With his foot to the metal, he eluded the posse and sped off deep into the heart of the city.

• • •

As a blood-orange sun rose in the east, dew covered the morning streets. Automobiles rushed down the boulevards and avenues. The smell of greasy breakfast filled the air. Aromas of tobacco wafted from cigar stores. Businessmen in hats and drab suits plodded along sidewalks on their way to Madison Avenue and Wall Street. They passed hobos begging for change. Some lounged in oversized black leather chairs while a shoe shiner buffed their footwear to a glaring sheen. Some bought papers from newsboys hawking the early edition of *The Clarion*.

"Extra! Extra! Read all about it! Phantom endangers innocent lives!"

The papers sold like candy bars. Soon the streets were littered with the tabloids. All over town the avenging angel's mug stared out from the front page.

• • •

Dan Fowler G-Man crinkled his leathery face at the whiff of evil still permeating the air at the bank. Dressed in a pressed blue suit and matching tie, he pushed back the gray hat covering his neatly combed hair. His black shoes were silent as he crossed the floor surveying the area.

Fowler, the bureau's two-fisted agent, mulled over the case as if he was a dog with a rawhide bone. There were too many peculiar things about this incident. The paper likened the scene to the O.K. Corral with innocent lives in jeopardy. The evidence indicated otherwise. Every crime scene spoke to him, and this one shouted from the rafters that the thieves' murderer was quiet, bloodless, and efficient.

He crouched down and poked at a burlap bag. It was clear to him that Slapsy was not responsible for the crime as the writer of *The Clarion* article had indicated. Whoever it was, based on the evidence on the burlap bag, was linked in some way to a farm. The ringleader could not be Stickpin, a city boy. Those two points swirling in his brain caused him to partially connect the dots.

Nicholas Spano popped into his mind and he couldn't erase the image. He pulled out a pad and scribbled the name. Spano, a wealthy businessman, had a large horse farm upstate.

Fowler's thoughts then turned to the Phantom Detective. What did the maverick know? Without exposing his cover story to the NYPD, somehow he would need to reach out to the hero.

• • •

Frank Havens was a man of powerful and virile stature, with a bulldog chin, stout build, and salt and pepper hair. He had built the news empire that was *The Clarion*. Using his wide-spread influence to fight crime, he served as a beacon in a world of darkness for the good citizens of New York City. This noble and lofty goal was the genesis of the mysterious crime fighter known as the Phantom Detective.

At the end of World War I, a troubled young man came to Havens. He had seen the horrors of battle, tasted the peril, and liked it!

Havens felt the best way to channel these tendencies in the youth was to encourage him to help others and to be a force for good in society. So he threw down the gauntlet to the high-spirited lad in the form of a suggestion. An article in *The Clarion* pointed to a killer whose identity was unknown. Frank told the young man to track down the murderer.

• • •

At the counter sat a thick, florid stubble-faced desk sergeant. With his shirt collar open, he was busy rubberstamping forms and doing other clerical work. He was an automaton who was so efficient that he didn't even look up when someone was talking to him to know what they needed or where they needed to go. He would either point or hand over a document and continue his work. But his next customer made sure he caught the man's attention.

A shadow blocked the sergeant's light and caused him to look up. His bored expression quickly changed to one of astonishment. A masked man wearing a military trench coat stood before him holding a shabby, despondent male by the back of the neck.

"Special delivery, Sergeant!"

"What in Samhain do you think you're doing?!" the policeman demanded.

Throwing the villain to the floor and putting his hand on him, the mask hero replied, "Bringing in the man responsible for the multiple heinous murders in the city! And you're welcome."

With that, the crusader kicked the man in the stomach and rapidly exited the station.

• • •

New York's mighty champion was a double-edged sword. To some he was their savior; to others his true motives were questionable. Frank did his best to convince the municipal movers and shakers that the covert paladin was on the side of right. Today that task proved to be more daunting.

In his enormous wood-paneled office, sitting at his mammoth marble-topped escritoire, he read the disparaging front page account of the Phantom Detective's latest foray into crime fighting. What angered him the most was that it appeared to be penned by his ace reporter, Steve Huston. Havens smelled a rat!

The further he read, the more pungent the odor. He knew all his employees, especially Steve, frontwards and backwards. The trusted scribe would not stoop to this kind of blatant yellow journalism. Someone must have planted the story.

As he folded the newspaper, his mental wheels began to spin. It would take all of his powers of persuasion to mollify the city officials. The atonal ring of his ornate phone was a welcome distraction. He cradled the receiver.

"Muriel!" he exclaimed. His features brightened as he heard his daughter's voice. Muriel Havens was the apple of his eye and the most coveted single woman in the city. With Frank's blessing, she was only interested in Richard Curtis Van Loan, wealthy, cosmopolitan playboy.

• • •

As Dan Fowler was about to leave, he pulled his hat brim low to shield his eyes from the sunlight coming in through the glass doors. Then he felt a presence. He whipped around. A figure clad head to toe in somber attire slinked toward the door. Dark glasses obscured his eyes.

Fowler quickly sized up the intruder. Broad shoulders indicated a male. Fluid movement signaled dexterity and he realized he was up against a formidable opponent.

"Stop!" Fowler demanded with authority.

The adversary tensed and then reflexes took over. The dark horse lunged fists first for the government operative. He'd seen that kind of fancy maneuvering by the Phantom Detective and countered with a sidestep. This wasn't the disguised hero, but someone just as lethal.

The figure recovered and squared off with the G-Man. Fowler slowed his breathing to a tactical tempo, allowing his mind to work more efficiently. He evaluated that the assailant had something to prove. Dan waited for his challenger to make a move.

The attacker stepped forward. The agent paced back ever so slightly. His aim was to pull his opponent in and catch him off balance. The man advanced. Fowler parried to the left and...*bammo!* The man's dome snapped back when the G-Man head-butted him. But that didn't take Fowler's aggressor down.

The sinister character threw a right cross which grazed Dan's temple as he ducked. The villain's knuckles were sharp, and the lawman could feel the blood trail down his cheek. He noticed something shiny and gory on assaulter's index finger, a silver skull ring. How could he have missed it?

Seeing an opening, the G-Man rushed the spook, thrusting his knee to his adversary's stomach. The man grunted and the pain caused him to retreat. With swift feet, he headed for the door.

Fowler drew his gun. He aimed for the perpetrator's leg and squeezed the trigger. The shot struck the man's calf. With extreme vigor, he did not miss a beat and flew through the door. Dan continued the chase.

The form ran along the sidewalk. Pedestrians were feather pillows as he tossed them out of the way. At one point, he hurled a poor damsel into the G-Man. Dan caught the frightened woman and planted her on the ground. He dodged a bystander and resumed his hot pursuit.

The G-Man's mark bolted across the street, stopped in the middle of the avenue, and flagged down a cab. He waited until Dan was upon him, then flung the door open into Fowler, knocking him off his feet. Winded, the agent jumped up flashing a gleaming shield at the cabby. He slammed the door and leaped onto the cab's running board. "Drive!"

The marauder moved rapidly along the sidewalk and then whipped around. A gun was in his fist and a flame spat from its barrel. Dan hunched low. The vehicle's front glass cracked and the cabby ducked.

Fowler straightened up and leaned against the vehicle. He fanned the hammer, and the barrel of his big pistol growled like a grizzly. The fugitive dodged the bullets whistling by his head. One bullet ricocheted off a lamp post and made a loud *clang*. The black-clad assailant turned into an alley. Dan barked at the cabby to follow. The taxi driver wrenched the wheel, skidded around the corner, and sped after the hoodlum. Fowler hooked his arm through the window and hung on.

The alley ended at a brick wall. Slamming on the brakes, the driver brought the taxi to screeching halt a couple feet in front of the runner. The man pressed himself against the wall. His breathing was shallow and audible as he pounced on the hood, leaping for a fire escape.

The G-Man jumped after him. He felt cabled muscles as he grabbed the ascending man's leg, who with beastly force threw the lawman into the air. Then, with the agility of a monkey, he climbed up the shaky ladder.

Fowler took flight, whirled and, with one hand, caught the lowest rung. He pitched upward like a trapeze artist and scrambled after the assailant. The figure wriggled through a partially open window. The agent reached out to grab him again, but the man shook free.

Through the glass Dan saw the fugitive run past an elderly couple, knocking over their dinner and disappearing into the apartment. The agent rapped on the pane and presented his badge. The terrified old man opened the window all the way. Dan stepped over the sill.

Just as the woman was about to say something, the G-Man held his finger to his lips. The couple ducked as he drew his piece. Silently, he crept around the apartment. He scoured every inch of the pad, finding no sign of the intruder. When he heard the old lady scream, he rushed back to the living room. The thug was holding the woman at gunpoint. The old man pleaded for his wife's life. Fowler took aim at the wayward man's head.

"Let her go, your fight's with me!" the G-Man ordered.

The man cackled. "You underestimate the value of innocent lives as bargaining chips! Drop the gun or the biddy gets it!"

Dan understood all too well the nature of evil. No matter how diabolical these cretins' minds were, they always made a mistake. There'd be a tiny slip-up that a trained agent could capitalize on. He lowered his gun slightly but didn't drop it, a compromising move designed to throw his opponent off-kilter.

The dark man started to waver. "I mean it, drop it!"

Dan lowered his gun even more and then crouched down as if he was going to place the pistol on the floor. As he did, the thug began to inch himself and the woman through the doorway. Fowler noticed he had relaxed his grip and let the weapon's barrel dangle. A mistake!

Although it was a gamble, it was the only chance the G-Man had at saving the woman. With amazing speed, he snatched a heavy glass ashtray off the coffee table, hurling it at the man's head. The goon instinctively ducked, but the object grazed his temple as it whizzed by. Throwing the woman to the floor, he pivoted around the corner of the doorframe. Fowler resumed the chase.

The fugitive led him through the grimy hallways and onto the rooftop, running with superhuman speed. Fowler was no slowpoke, but he was beginning to feel his limits.

The man in black came to edge of the roof. He stood on the ledge, looked at the agent, then let himself fall. Dan raced over and peered down. Nothing.

He searched high and low under the ledge and didn't find a thing, muttering curses that his adversary had bested him. The G-Man and escape artist would meet again on another urban battle field.

• • •

Slapsy McCoy stood at a full-length mirror while his tailor fitted him for a suit. Even the dark pinstripe jacket couldn't hide his corpulence. Generous amounts of pomade tried to tame black hair over his balding scalp. Red-blossomed puffy cheeks signified copious amount of drink and complimented his broccoli nose. His eyes bulged, ready to burst like grapes.

A ruffian shining Slapsy's shoes had to dodge his feet when he shook like he had Saint Vitus dance. Gripping a newspaper, he almost shredded the rag. He frothed at the mouth as he pointed to the tabloid. This was the same headline that caught the attention of Frank Havens.

With all the commotion, the tailor accidentally stuck his boss with a pin. Slapsy, in a pent-up rage, turned to the underling. He took a cleansing breath. The seamster stood stoically and braced himself for the anticipated punishment.

"Don't worry, it happens," Slapsy reassured him, before continuing to stare incredulously at the newsprint. "Can you believe this? Look at this!" He shoved the tabloid into the hands of a well-dressed and manicured man, Jonny Olivetti, Slapsy's counselor. The tall advisor scrutinized the daily and furrowed his long brow. His dark eyes glistened as his lips moved ever so slightly reading the story.

Slapsy grew impatient. "Come on, it's not *War and Peace*! Hurry it up!"

The snappily dressed consultant folded the paper and tucked it under his arm. He calmly looked at the mobster. Slapsy's face turned crimson. Everyone else in the room fidgeted at the sight of the stand-off.

"Well, what do you make of it?" Slapsy demanded.

Olivetti cleared his throat and touched the bandage on the side of his temple. "It is quite clear that someone is trying to frame you."

The crooked chieftain wagged his finger. "Exactly, and it's clear they didn't do their homework. Stickpin hasn't worked for me in a long time, and he'd never scream for his mommy! I know for certain his mother beat the tears out of him at a very young age!"

With only half his pants completed, Slapsy walked away from the tailor and over to the plate glass window, not caring that his boxers hung in the breeze. He looked back at his entourage.

"If I thought I had a rat in the house, one of you'd already be dead." His gaze shifted to Olivetti's wound. "Make sure that thing doesn't get infected!"

The others relaxed a little. He stared out at the city. Down below, the cars looked like fireflies flitting back and forth. He gazed at the streets as if he'd find some inspiration in the abyss. But there was none.

"I got two thorns in my side. The Phantom Detective and an enemy who has not yet shown himself!" Slapsy balled his fists and gritted his teeth like he was going to explode.

Olivetti's lips formed a pursed smile.

• • •

A blue, smoky haze filled the room of city big wigs seated at a large varnished oak table. It was a lavishly appointed space where framed art hung on the walls and leather-bound volumes filled the shelves. A lamp hanging over the table was the only light in an otherwise dark area. Men puffed their stogies as they anxiously shifted in red padded chairs.

At the head of the table was Mayor Dewey, a distinguished man in his early fifties with an athletic build. Seated next to him was Commissioner Warren. To the Commissioner's left was the chunky, red-faced Captain McGrath. At the far end of the table, Frank Havens sat in thoughtful repose.

"So, am I to understand that you are here to catch Slapsy McCoy?" asked Frank.

All heads turned to Dan Fowler, standing at the other end of the table. "Since it's a bank robbery, I've been ordered to take over the case. And, regrettably, I am also instructed to arrest the Phantom Detective."

Havens frowned at the thought of the Phantom Detective being hunted by G-men.

Seated across from the Captain, Inspector Gregg said, "I'm pretty sure we can handle Slapsy, Commissioner!" McGrath and Gregg exchanged quizzical looks.

Commissioner Warren threw up his hands. "Sorry, men, there's nothing I can do. Like it or not, when Washington gives orders, we must obey."

To no avail the Inspector and Captain grumbled further protests.

Dan Fowler walked to the other side of the room. "Washington has lost patience with the Phantom Detective. They frown upon a vigilante putting innocent lives in danger. He's becoming a menace and, he, as well as Slapsy, needs to be stopped. Based on the newspaper story, it is quite clear you need my help. Let me assure you all, I have every intention of involving the NYPD in this case."

"Agent Fowler, with all due respect, you know the Phantom Detective would never do anything to endanger the innocent people of our city. The account that you read in my paper is false, and the story has been retracted. We are releasing the facts tomorrow," Frank Havens said.

The FBI agent gave the news mogul a sympathetic nod.

The Mayor cleared his throat. "Gentlemen, at this point I do not see a downside to allowing Agent Fowler to assist us in capturing these two villains."

Frank Havens held back his anger and quietly composed himself. In his line of work, it was important to maintain control of his emotions.

"...you are here to catch Slapsy McCoy?'

What upset him the most was that, contrary to what was being said, the Mayor was grateful to the Phantom Detective as was everybody else.

Havens had backed the city official financially and had given him a hearty endorsement in *The Clarion*. Mayor Dewey made the election promise that he would defend the actions of the Phantom Detective.

It wasn't that Frank was blind to the pickle Dewey found himself in, but the mayor didn't have to cave without protest. Maybe it was time for Dewey to go but Havens had reservations about the young challenger in the upcoming mayoral race; there was something oily about his character and presentation.

• • •

Gathered in Central Park amongst the lush greenery, an ocean of people listened to the peppery rhetoric coming from the grandstand. When there was a pause in the speech, they thundered their applause and chanted "Help is on the way!"

The slogan was Robert O'Brien's war cry. O'Brien, the blond, tanned young man with pearly white teeth standing at the microphone, was the mayor's tough, starry-eyed challenger. His straw boater with the red, white, and blue band perched rakishly on his head. The scarlet braces holding up his pressed blue pants gave him a Clarence Darrow appeal. And his rolled up shirt sleeves augmented his image of a fighter.

Behind him stood a line of several dignified men wearing duplicate attire – his staff. They nodded their heads like the "yes men" they were. Like a general reviewing his troops, Robert O'Brien worked the stage and surveyed the crowd.

"You are all the recipients of Mayor Dewey's promises!" he shouted. The crowd chanted his slogan. Bob paced to the other side of the podium and then stopped, taking a pregnant pause. Tension whipped through the audience as they waited for more wisdom.

"Correction! You are all the benefactors of Mayor Dewey's broken promises and failed policies!" Again the faithful congregation affirmed his statement. When the multitude calmed down, he moved again to the center of the stage and took a messianic stance.

"Dewey has brought this wonderful city of ours corruption, graft, and crime!"

The politician patted the front of his coat and checked his inside pocket. He then turned to his staff. One of his suited lemmings ran toward him waving a white handkerchief like it was a flag of surrender. The young ideologue snatched it, removed his hat, and mopped his forehead. He let the cloth dangle between his index and middle fingers, waiting for it to be removed. A staffer promptly disposed of the soiled rag.

O'Brien placed the silver microphone on its stand. He pointed to the stage with its stars and stripes motif. "The decoration on this platform represents who I am, an American! And it is un-American for someone like Mayor Dewey, holding the most prominent position in this city, to let you all live in fear and suffer in squalor! To make matters worse, the mayor is sympathetic to a bloodthirsty masked madman who puts innocent lives in danger!" O'Brien held up the edition of *The Clarion*. "But not I! I grew up roaming the mean streets of Hell's Kitchen! So trust me, I know how to fight and I. Will. Fight. For. You! Help is on the way!" Robert gesticulated with the rolled up newspaper and conducted a frenzied symphony of the mantra.

The thousands clapped their hands and jumped up and down, continuing to shout. Their numbers appeared to go on for miles. Somewhere in the back, a black Rolls Royce was parked at the edge of the park.

The luxurious sedan belonged to the mystery billionaire, Nicholas Spano. The passenger window behind the driver lowered. A plume of gray smoke emanated from the darkness.

• • •

A yellow moon shone on the G-Man's face. He crouched beside a long rail fence running the circumference of the most expensive piece of land in all of New York State. Across the vast plain were the glaring lights of the extravagant domain. This was the home of Nicholas Spano.

As Fowler took in the surroundings, he thought about how impressive these grounds would look in the daylight. But at night the mansion appeared to be an ominous, reclining giant. The surrounding trees stood like hulks guarding the slumbering beast.

Earlier that day at the rally, Dan got close to Robert O'Brien. As he shook his hand, he slipped a listening and tracking device in the side pocket of the man's blazer. The signal led to the rolling estate of the financier. While investigating at the bank with his portable crime lab, he detected traces of a special grain in the burlap bag. Grain fed to the billionaire's Arabian horses. A possible connection?

Since his name kept popping up in other cases, the FBI director had ordered an investigation of the young politician. Fowler gleaned from the files that O'Brien had been on the board of Dracon Chemicals which was, coincidentally, a subsidiary of Nicholas Spano enterprises. As a result of this connection, Dan had been assigned to do an aggressive investigation of the political challenger. Spano's tentacles reached deep inside the metropolis. In order not to tip off Spano of the investigation, he concocted a phony story about wanting to kill two birds with one stone by capturing Slapsy McCoy and arresting the Phantom Detective.

In actuality, Washington was more than happy to have the masked detective on their side, often providing resources for the hero. As for Slapsy, New York's finest could handle that piker all by themselves. Any thought spent on McCoy would be a waste of the agent's time. When it was right, he would bring the Phantom in on the case. But now he had to pick up more intel on the doings of Spano and O'Brien.

So now he found himself pressed against the fence with headphones plugged into a receiver.

As the hours passed, Fowler grew impatient. So far all he had heard was O'Brien's arrival at the estate and his banal conversation with the domestic help. But Dan knew he had to persevere. Something nefarious was afoot. His instincts were sensitive to this notion. So, he waited, enduring the oppressive heat and the discomfort of gnats and mosquitoes buzzing around his head.

Persistence paid off when he heard a thick timbered door slam shut. He concluded that O'Brien must be in the magnate's study and that Spano had just entered. He was right! Through the crackling static he heard the accented rasp of the cabalistic tycoon.

"Ah yes, Mr. O'Brien, how nice of you to join us!" Spano said.

The word "us" intrigued the agent. Was there another person in the room? Dan thought he had heard more than one pair of footsteps enter. Now his suspicions were confirmed.

• • •

A candelabra provided the only illumination in the study. But the five candles were enough to light the area, giving it a shadowy appearance. Black leather books stood at attention on floor to ceiling shelves. A mounted tiger head stared down defiantly at those who entered this lair. A leather brass-studded sofa rested on one side of the room facing two matching chairs. Near the bay window, which looked out into the abyss was a big black gilded desk. Behind this large piece of furniture sat a man with sallow complexion. He was the infamous Nicholas Spano. He puffed an ivory pipe as he peered at the young O'Brien seated on the sofa.

"Mr. Olivetti informs us that Dan Fowler is in town," Spano said, clearing his throat. He gazed into a dark corner and summoned the counselor as though he were charming a viper out of a basket.

Olivetti materialized, a serpentine curl of smoke escaping his lips. His fingers clenched a long cigarette. The bandage, still plastered to his temple, detracted from the dapper effect of his shark skin suit. Other than that he was all slither.

"I had a scuffle with that flatfoot at the bank. We may want to accelerate our plans."

O'Brien fidgeted. He had never wanted to get in this deep, but ambition had gotten the better of him. The seduction of receiving unlimited resources and a big campaign war chest, courtesy of Nicholas Spano, was too tempting.

Spano let loose a hissing laugh. "My sources in the NYPD have informed me that Agent Fowler is on the trail of Slapsy McCoy and the Phantom. How are you doing with Slapsy, Olivetti?"

"Slapsy is coming apart at the seams."

"Good, we'll let Fowler take care of the Phantom."

O'Brien gulped nervously. "I saw Fowler at my rally… He shook hands with me…"

Spano arched an eyebrow and gave Olivetti a piercing look. With the grace of a swordsman, Olivetti moved swiftly across the room. He grabbed the candidate roughly and frisked him. When O'Brien tried to protest the harsh treatment, the slimy operative clamped his mouth shut. After a thorough search, he found what he was looking for; the small device!

"Fowler is onto us!" Olivetti barked.

Spano spun in his chair and surveyed the vast lawn. "Alert security! Light up the grounds! I want this interloper alive!"

• • •

Fowler tensed. When he heard the crushing sound in his headphones, he realized something was wrong. Someone had detected the device.

Bright beacons lit up the real estate. The sound of barking came deep from the throats of a pack of creatures. Bloodhounds! Fowler didn't have much time. The animals would be on him in seconds. If he didn't get away, they'd turn him into a sanguine side of beef.

As Fowler ran, the tortured yelping grew louder. He turned his head and saw swinging lamplights trail after him. His car was just over the hill. So close, but yet so far! With small steps he sprinted up the knoll, dodging branches and underbrush. Then he heard a menacing growl. Needle sharp teeth pierced through the skin of his ankle.

With shutter-like speed, he drew his weapon and bashed the beast's head with the butt of the gun. The dog whimpered and then went still. The move startled the herd below. The handler and the horde then recovered. Fowler leaped when a shot popped near his foot. He swung around the closest tree and ducked for cover. More shots rang out.

Taking a deep breath, the agent peered from behind the trunk and returned fire. He heard another anguished cry and winced at the thought of killing an animal. Firing two more shots, he dashed from his cover and continued his climb.

He dove over the crest of the hill. The car was a welcome sight. He slid over the hood. Opening the door, he jumped in. When the engine kicked to life, he raced down the road to safety.

His thoughts troubled him as he drove. Something big and disastrous was about to happen. He wished he'd been able to ascertain more from his listening post. The urgency of the situation demanded he seek the help and resources of the Phantom Detective.

• • •

A shadow skulked along the walls as it made its way through the labyrinth of municipal building halls. The intruder did his best to move with secrecy, but the clink of his bulky cargo echoed through the cavernous passage ways. Every time he made a noise, he briefly stopped and waited.

When he was sure he hadn't been detected, he continued his silent trek. Three doors down he reached his destination. Clacking footsteps caused his muscles to constrict. He drew a gun from a shoulder holster.

A beam of light, like a reptilian tongue, darted at the walls of the corridor. The figure cocked his snub nose. He relaxed when he heard whistling knowing the security guard was not on the alert.

After pausing a few minutes, he crouched down and set his delicate burden on the floor. The criminal cringed when the package made a *thud*. He lifted the lading gently and set it down again. This time it made no sound. Satisfied, he pulled out a special tool, picked the lock, and snuck in to Mayor Dewey's office.

With one hand, he shined his flashlight around the office; another den of power. In the crook of his other arm was the item he was to deliver; a bomb!

Its casing was a black, steel Dutch oven. In it was dynamite and a very flammable substance called Hydra, a super-powered petroleum jelly made specifically for the U.S. military by Dracon Chemicals. The government, however, had found it too unstable for their use and had denied the company the contract.

The intruder set the explosive gizmo on the long wooden table. He lifted the lid, reached in, and wound a small red alarm clock mounted to the contraption's volatile guts. The clock would trigger a hammer, striking flint. The spark from the flint would then ignite the fuse coiled around the inside of the pot, connected to the dynamite. The resulting explosion would unleash the hell that was Hydra!

Once the alarm sounded, the terrorist would have just enough time to vacate the building. When the man was finished setting this horror in motion, he swiftly made for the door.

The subversive left behind his torch which cast an alien pallor on the cauldron. Coming from inside was the ominous tick of the time piece. After fifteen minutes, the loud jangle of the alarm rang. A thud was followed by the crackle of the fuse. The kettle rumbled as the spark burned the wick. As the cooking chamber exploded, shrapnel filled the air and blew the flashlight into the wall. Mixed with the metal shavings were flaming gobs of gel. Fiery, semi-solid substance spilled from the wrecked crockery onto the floor. In a few moments blazing red rivers crossed each other. They ignited the desk, the couch, and all of the other trappings. The flaming streams flowed to the office entrance and licked the wood of the door. In no time at all, the egress crumbled like filament.

The roving, ghastly pyre made its way into the hall. Bubbling, it burst into seven dragon heads. A giant fire ball flew from each mouth, rolling in every direction and leaving destruction in its path.

City Hall was an overbearing, solid concrete structure. Who would have guessed it would be vulnerable to attack? Tiny explosions grew louder as if some terrifying force was making its way to the forefront. The glass doors shattered and blew off their hinges, windows burst. The sky rained fire and glass. Flames spewed from every opening. A thick cloud of black, ugly smoke blocked out the starry night.

• • •

A red, white, and blue banner with several hanging identical pennants stretched the length of the great hall. It read: "Re-elect Mayor Thomas Dewey! He'll hold the line and guide us to a better place!"

Soothing music came from a tuxedoed orchestra. The wealthy and influential, dressed in formal wear, held each other as they slid across the polished dance floor to those satisfying sounds. Other luminaries huddled with their cocktails. Some were making backroom deals. Yet others discussed strategy for re-electing the incumbent.

Many of them picked finger sandwiches off silver platters the waiters palmed as they flitted though the crowd. No gathering was complete without conversation about the exploits of the Phantom Detective. The opinions of the group were divided on which side the vanquisher fell.

In the middle of the dance floor moved a graceful, young couple. The man spun and then dipped her when it was appropriate to do so. The pair was Muriel Havens and Richard Curtis Van Loan.

Muriel was a brilliant redhead whose shapely figure complimented Van Loan's broad-shouldered build, sandy hair, and sturdy features. His capable hands brought out the best in the news mogul's daughter as he augmented her expert dance moves with skillful maneuvering.

As the twosome floated across the dance floor, Muriel noticed Richard's faraway look. She waved her hand in front of his face. "Dreaming again are you, buster?"

Van Loan snapped out of his reverie and focused on his feisty companion. "Sorry, I was preoccupied."

Muriel rolled her eyes. Richard Curtis Van Loan was her beau, and she loved him very much; but oftentimes grew frustrated with his 'devil-may-care attitude'. She didn't mind his lazy approach to life, but she saw a diamond in the rough that, with some polish and care, she could turn into a crown jewel.

Van Loan's preoccupation had nothing to do with apathy. His instincts sensed trouble. He felt a tremor that he was sure no one else could detect. He had honed these instincts in the Great War. Having been exposed to constant danger and seeing the carnage of battle, his nerves were raw. Something terrible had just happened in the city. He could feel it.

"I'm sorry, honey, I guess I drifted off momentarily. It won't happen again."

Muriel kissed him on the cheek. "It better not, if you know what's good for you. This campaign is very important to my father, and he is counting on all of our support."

Van Loan smiled. "It's important to me, too. So is your dad."

He and Muriel continued to dance. She gazed at the man before her and hoped one day he would make an honest woman out of her. The playboy's face projected something that caused Muriel to take pause. It was an expression of fierce, iron determination, so unlike the easygoing cosmopolitan. What Muriel did not know was that Van Loan was hiding another identity…the Phantom Detective. Van Loan wanted to tell her about his crusade against crime, but for her own safety his alter ego must remain a secret. The city's well-being took priority over his feelings for her. This was a reality with which he was very comfortable.

As the festivities continued late into the night, the feeling of danger gnawed at him. The Phantom began to take over.

"Are you sure you're all right?" Muriel asked.

Van Loan smiled and kissed her on the cheek. "I'm fine, dear."

Muriel shot him a skeptical look. "I'm not so sure about that. When your disposition changes like this, I know something's troubling you."

Richard Van Loan shook his head and flashed his normal designer smile. "Nothing to worry about. I love you, Muriel." But the threatening sensation would not go away and his hunger for action grew.

"I wonder if Mayor Dewey is here yet?" he asked.

"Father said he would be late. He told him he had to attend to some pressing city business."

Muriel's reply concerned Van Loan. What could be so urgent? The festivities were interrupted when a disheveled Dewey staffer came rushing onto the dance floor.

"There's a fire at City Hall!"

A murmur rippled through the crowd as people grew agitated.

Van Loan grabbed Muriel and knifed his way through the crowd. He must get to the scene!

• • •

As the fire continued to consume the structure, firemen did their best to douse the conflagration. But, as hard as they tried, the fire was winning.

Bystanders in the street dodged the sparks and braved the ash falling all around them. The frightful wildfire mesmerized them. Sirens signified more police and emergency vehicles were headed toward the scene.

Richard Curtis Van Loan stood in front of Muriel watching the burning wreckage. By now the Phantom Detective had completely taken over his persona, and this was no accident.

People jumped and gasped when they saw the building buckle. Precinct blue coats pushed the crowd further away from the inferno.

Van Loan moved with the crowd to a safer distance, but his eyes were still on the building. With his exceptional powers of observation, he noticed a baleful shadow shaped like a dragon's head in the flames. He turned when he heard someone shout.

"Look at the steps!"

Van Loan ventured over and saw an inscription in the stone: "Burn in hell, New York. Best regards, the Phantom Detective and Slapsy McCoy." It was urgent that he get to the bottom of this mystery.

"...Van Loan stood in front of Muriel..."

"What an awful thing to happen, especially during Mayor Dewey's campaign," Muriel interjected.

Van Loan looked at her with a grave expression. "Awful indeed! It's going to cause a major controversy for him, especially if people think the Phantom Detective was responsible for this."

Muriel grabbed Van Loan's jacket sleeve. "It can't be the Phantom behind this. Both you and I know that. We must get to father as quickly possible so we can warn him about the brewing trouble!"

"Yes, Muriel. Now, I must hail you a cab and take my leave."

Muriel looked at him in astonishment. "What do you need to do that's more important than going to see my father at *The Clarion*?"

Richard Van Loan gave Muriel a determined look. "You have to trust me. There is something I must do. I will call Frank later!"

"I do trust you. But you better have a good explanation for me next time I see you."

• • •

The prosperous lothario switched on the light and illuminated the living room of his penthouse. The apartment's decorations told the tale of Richard Curtis Van Loan.

Polo trophies lined the shelves. Tiger and lion heads from exotic and dangerous safaris to the Dark Continent were mounted proudly on the wall. A bear skin rug covered the center of the marble floor, and over it dangled an enormous crystal chandelier. But nothing in the apartment revealed anything about his other existence.

Van Loan tossed his jacket on the sofa and walked over to the large plate glass window. The outline of the Clarion building stood stalwart but dark in the city skyline. He would wait all night if had to, to see what he needed to see. The thrill of the mystery was rising inside him like mercury.

Drumming his fingers on the glass, he stood anxious, hoping. Then it came – the beacon!

As he saw the signal, Van Loan's face brightened for this was the Phantom Detective's call to arms. Richard stepped away from the window.

In his roomy sleeping chamber he stood in front of an enormous wardrobe. When he opened the door, a black trunk with brass rivets stared at him. Reaching down, he gripped the leather handles and hefted the chest onto a carved wood table, unlocking it and flipping open the top.

The contents contained various jars of makeup, hair gels, fake mustaches, skull caps, a very complete disguise kit. Tonight, as with all other nights when the services of the masked guardian were summoned, he would transform himself into Mr. Grey. This fictitious character was created to provide aid and counsel to Frank Havens when he sought the help of the Phantom. It was a protection for them both.

Gradually, Van Loan's appearance altered from the strapping, vigorous young man to the ashen, gray-haired elder. When the transformation was complete, he picked up the phone on the nightstand and dialed the number of *The Clarion* reception desk.

"*The Clarion* answering service," said the voice on the other end.

"Yes, please get word to Frank Havens that Mr. Grey will be calling on him at midnight tonight. Thank you."

• • •

"Read 'em and weep." Slapsy sat at a poker table, raked in his winnings, and blasted smoke on the pile of chips. He was in a jovial mood. Tonight the cards were his friends.

A music combo played some big band jazz while men in suits flung dice across the green felt of a Craps table. The Roulette wheel enchanted another circle of compulsive gamblers. Women in slinky gowns worked the room. Some carried cigarette trays while others solicited companionship.

A black checkered floor hosted those with happy feet as they laughed and danced the latest hops. While the partiers shuffled across the turf, hard core drinkers huddled over glasses of booze at the bar.

Sour expressions afflicted Slapsy's fellow players who were having a run of bad luck. Hanging off McCoy were two sultry dames, a blonde and brunette. Both cheered on cue when Slapsy gathered more loot. The crime boss would slip each a chip after every winning hand to show what a generous guy he was.

The din grew louder until it became a crescendo with an even louder boom. The door burst open and in came the law, all hands on a metal pole.

Everyone screamed as plain clothes detectives filed in following the men in blue. Inspector Gregg held his shield high so all could see it dazzling in the light. The head flatfoot walked over and pulled Slapsy up by the scruff of his neck and personally hooked the steel bracelets on his wrists.

"Patrick Jameson McCoy, I hereby place you under arrest for masterminding the robbery of State Bank and Trust as well as planting the bomb at City Hall."

Slapsy puffed up in rage as his face turned scarlet. "This is a frame job! I want a lawyer!"

Gregg lifted Slapsy's chin. "You'll get your lawyer…that and more!"

Two cops built like houses grabbed the portly kingpin and hustled him roughly out the door. The remaining patrons of the illegal afterhours joint stood against the wall with their hands up.

A uniform cop covered his face and took a nightstick to the bar, shattering the glass. The gaming tables were spilt in two and reduced to kindling by other lawmen swinging sledgehammers. Inspector Gregg studied the damage with a smile of satisfaction.

• • •

Richard Curtis Van Loan, disguised as Mr. Grey, traipsed through the charred remains of City Hall. He looked around briefly and envisioned himself in army greens, head covered by a steel pot helmet, clutching a Garand. He missed the war. Then, shaking his head, he refocused on the task at hand.

The soot and acrid odor made it necessary to cover his face with a handkerchief. He had to move quickly. A patrolman passing by might check in on the scene. So he stepped as quietly as possible through the rubble.

As the Phantom Detective, his keen investigative abilities had been set into motion. Any clue, be it big or small, could be the difference in cracking this conundrum. Very thoroughly he scanned the site, taking in every detail, smelling every odor, and listening for every unusual sound. Something here would provide answers to this heinous act. Tenacity paid off for the super sleuth.

He had made his way to what used to be the mayor's office. It was here he deduced that the bomb was placed, based on the evidence of metal shavings. But that wasn't the tell-tale clue. Stuck in what was left of the wall was what appeared to be a policeman's flashlight. The camouflaged investigator, with a gloved hand, picked it out of the damaged cement. He would hand this over to the G-Man who he was sure to be seeing soon.

• • •

The impressive door to Frank's office opened. In walked Mr. Grey. The dim light did nothing to accentuate his features. Havens stood behind his desk and extended a welcoming gesture to the gentleman. Seated in a plush chair was Dan Fowler. He gave the elder a curious stare. Mr. Grey shot back a sly smile. Then he slipped on his mask and became the Phantom Detective once more.

Havens took in the secret gumshoe's dirty clothes. "It looks as though you've been digging around at the crime scene already. So I'm pretty sure you know why I called you."

The Phantom Detective nodded, then reached into his pocket and produced the battered flashlight. He handed it to Fowler. "I found this at the scene."

The G-Man took it and marveled at the piece of tarnished evidence. "Police light, very interesting."

"I'm guessing you are coming to the same conclusion that I am," the Phantom replied. "The perpetrator is either connected to law enforcement or a night watchman."

Frank Havens chuckled at the irony of that last comment.

Fowler handed the torch back to the Phantom. "I would investigate it, but I think I'll wait and see what you come up with!"

The Phantom Detective stuffed the light in his pocket. "I can get the prints off it at my crime lab, but all I will be doing is confirming what I know!"

Frank stepped out from behind the desk, went over to the wet bar, and poured a drink from one of the many carafes of fine liquor perched in the cabinet. He took a gulp and swirled the ice with a fancy stir stick.

"As Dan was saying before you arrived, he has proof that both the bombing and the robbery are linked to the O'Brien campaign and Nicholas Spano."

"I partially overheard their plans the other night when I was on surveillance at Spano's horse farm."

The Phantom Detective nodded. "That would make sense since the substance used in the bomb was definitely Hydra!"

"And you know this how?" Havens asked.

The cloaked crusader pivoted toward Frank. "With a trained eye such as mine, I saw the shadow of the dragon's head in the flames at City Hall. It had to be Hydra. My examination of the light will prove that the perpetrator is connected to Dracon Chemicals, a subsidiary of Spano Enterprises."

"Why don't you check out that angle. In the meantime I'll go over to O'Brien's campaign headquarters and try to get some information out of the contender," Fowler suggested.

"Be careful, Phantom. The whole city thinks you were responsible for the bombing. I don't want to see you accidentally getting shot by a trigger-happy policeman," Havens said.

The Phantom acknowledged the comment with a nod. "There is bound to be chaos in the streets. O'Brien won't let this current crisis go to waste!"

• • •

"Like a phoenix rising from the ashes, this city will rise again and be the shining jewel of this country!" Columns of angry citizens stretched for miles along the major thoroughfares of the metropolis. In their pumping fists were placards trumpeting slogans that demanded action and called for the head of the Phantom Detective.

The parade of pandemonium ended at the ruined steps of city hall. At the crest, Robert O'Brien stood with one hand clenched in the air and a giant megaphone clutched in the other, he delivered another impassioned speech.

"I can't hear you!" came a shout from the crowd.

"But I can hear you!" O'Brien retorted. "And come Election Day Mayor Dewey's going to hear you!"

The multitude of frenzied followers cheered.

"And rest assured your tax dollars will go to work building the best city hall this town has ever had! We will have the strongest police force, best fire department, and greatest schools! And then we can arrest that shadowy vigilante known as the Phantom Detective who puts all of our lives at risk and who acts only for his own gain! Help is on the way!"

The chant reverberated throughout the city like a minor earthquake.

• • •

Dan Fowler walked through the doors of the nondescript storefront. Tables cluttered with phones, letters, and envelopes filled the room. Some chairs were tucked neatly under the tables while others had been pulled out haphazardly. Campaign posters decorated the walls, and big red, white, and blue buntings hung from the ceiling. Fowler looked around the room and deduced that everyone had dropped what they were doing and hurried off to participate in the impromptu rally. He and the Phantom had to act fast. They agreed that an even bigger act of terror was sure to follow. A man as evil as Nicholas Spano couldn't help himself.

He stepped into a back office, which was most likely O'Brien's. The room was sparsely decorated. Fowler paused at a roll-top desk. The purpose of the meager furnishings was intentional to create an image that the candidate was a man of the people.

Papers were neatly organized on a blotter. The agent glanced over his shoulder and then proceeded to thumb through one of the stacks. On a thick bonded sheet was a crudely drawn city street map with Medical Triage Centers written at the top. Red stars were glued strategically on the diagram indicating the locations. This piqued Fowler's interest. He folded and discreetly tucked the piece of evidence in his jacket pocket.

"Can I help you?"

Fowler spun to discover Jonny Olivetti standing in the doorway, a clean white bandage taped to his forehead.

The G-Man brandished his badge. "FBI... I was hoping to catch candidate O'Brien in his office to find out if he had any insight on who might be responsible for the bombing."

Olivetti let out a condescending laugh. "Isn't it obvious who's behind it? What more do you need besides a personal message in graffiti by those responsible?"

Dan Fowler smiled. "You might be right, but have you ever had the feeling that someone was trying to put one over on you? I mean it's almost like this was too easy."

Fowler was using one of his investigative tricks: get the suspect to actively involve himself in the case. Oftentimes murderers and other criminals unwittingly confess to their deeds, or at least give up something that can be used to incriminate them.

"It's possible they aren't that smart," Olivetti contributed.

When Fowler stepped closer, he could sense the slick operator's uneasiness. It then registered this could be the man with whom he had the altercation at the bank. "I would be more willing to accept that assumption if the perpetrators had used something simple like a stick of dynamite. But we've determined that the device used took time and planning and that it contained a highly specialized ingredient made only by a specific company."

Olivetti fidgeted.

"You wouldn't know anything about Dracon Chemicals, would you?"

The slimy consultant's face flushed. "Mr. O'Brien is holding an emergency press conference. I will be happy to tell him you were here."

"You do that! Oh, just one more thing; I like that snazzy bandage on your forehead. What happened?"

Olivetti gritted his teeth. He didn't like being bested and angrily showed the agent to the door. Fowler had enough evidence to arrest him, and Spano as well. But right now a higher purpose called; saving the city from more destruction!

• • •

A buzzing fence surrounded the ominous structure of Dracon Chemicals. Behind that deterrent was another one, a foreboding wall manned by uniformed sentries. Spotlights assaulted the inky sky and thick forest.

The Phantom crouched along the tree line and stared at the explosives factory. His analysis of the flashlight had revealed that the miscreant who planted the bomb was indeed a night watchman at Dracon Chemicals. That incriminating clue was all the justification he needed to do what he was about to do. Normally, he would make a citizen's arrest of those responsible for a crime. But this was an extreme situation. And extreme situations called for even more drastic measures.

Tonight, the disguise of choice was that of a Dracon security guard. Through nefarious connections, Frank Havens had supplied him with a manifest of the company's security personnel. He purposely picked an employee, received access to the individual's corporate dossier, and then concocted his ruse.

Although he looked like the employee, he had no way to replicate the voice. He knew it wouldn't take long for the guard at the gate to see through his deception. The gatekeeper would then have to be neutralized. The Phantom would do his best to preserve life, but instances like these were fluid and anything could happen.

Reaching into his bag, he pulled out vial of green luminescent substance. This brew had been developed at his secret lab and was designed to destroy the big vats of Hydra.

A few yards ahead of him was the guard shack, protecting the entrance to the factory. The champion sauntered up to the security guard who was on duty. The gatekeeper's face was deformed by a giant bluish scar. The blemish ran down his right cheek to the prominent cleft in his square chin. The Phantom looked into the man's menacing eyes and waited for acknowledgement.

When the guard saw the man he thought was his relief, he put down the evening edition of *The Clarion* and lifted his bulky frame off the chair.

"Mac! You're early!" he observed. Then he looked at the imposter with a cooler eye. "Something wrong, bub?"

The Detective shrugged his shoulders.

"Can't you talk?"

The Phantom stepped back.

"Hey, something ain't right here!"

With a quicksilver motion, the Phantom hurled a right cross to the lug's jaw. His fist hit bone, and the masked avenger felt as if he'd punched granite. The sentry went cross-eyed, but stayed upright. The hero did not let him fully recover. He grabbed the man's neck and squeezed hard. The guard's peepers rolled to the back of his head and he flopped to the turf. The Phantom dragged him inside the gatehouse. Time was of the essence! Someone was bound to check in and it wouldn't be long before the security breach would be discovered.

Making his way across the yard, the Phantom headed for an open door and went in. Inside the factory, the drone of machinery beat on his ear drums. A network of catwalks caught his eye; a great vantage point to launch his assaults! He spied a ladder and scurried up to one of the tiers.

When he reached the top, he inched along the bridge. Below him were cooling tanks and processing equipment. Giant tubes connected the machinery to the vats of Hydra.

The cloaked vanquisher pulled out the tube of antidote, popped the cork, and carefully poured the liquid into the molten gunk. He cautiously moved along the scaffolding, pulled out another container from his bag, and repeated the process at another vat, and then another. The heat from the vats began to melt his makeup, and he felt it running down his face. With no other option, he donned his domino mask. When he was sure he neutralized all of the vats, he pulled a rope out of his satchel, tied it to the rail, and shimmied down to ground level.

He proceeded to plant charges at the base of each vat. When he had finished securing the last one, he breathed a sigh of relief. The explosives attached to timers were set to go off long after he had gone.

"Hey, pal, whaddya think you're doing!?"

The Phantom made an about-face to another burly worker.

"It's the Phantom Detective! Get him!" he yelled above the din of machinery. The factory hand ran to a nearby wall and pulled a lever. An obnoxious alarm wailed.

"Attention all personnel! Intruder alert! Intruder alert! The Phantom Detective is on the premises!"

The vigilante dashed to the man who had sounded the alarm. The goon took off and swung his metal hard hat, striking the Phantom across his face. The hero reeled back. The Dracon employee lunged, knocking him off balance. Before his attacker could do any more damage, the Phantom Detective drove a foot into the man's solar plexus. The assailant was propelled backward and hit the concrete. The winded worker tried to rise, but the Phantom gave him a karate chop to the neck which ended the altercation.

The crime fighter drew his pistol and took cover behind a mixing machine. The Phantom saw gobs of grease oozing down the sides and winced at the pungent smell.

He spied armed security guards flooding the main floor. Taking aim, he trained his pistol on one of the sentries. Seeing Thompsons, it was evident that he was outgunned. His only chance of survival would be to even the odds. But how?

If he were to shoot and kill only one, he would be ventilated by machine gun fire. When the armed gunmen started to search for him, the Phantom knew his only option would be to silently incapacitate one of them and commandeer his weapon. That would give the masked hero a chance to mow down as many as he had to and make a break for freedom.

When the first assailant came upon him, he flipped his gun around and cold-cocked him. After he grabbed the man's machine gun, he stepped out in the open, and squeezed the trigger letting the bullets fan out. Taken by surprise, the guards hopped around like Mexican jumping beans and then dropped to the floor. Some recovered and sought protection behind the machinery, returning fire.

As the Phantom responded with more gunfire, he slowly inched his way toward a side exit. He fired two more shots and rushed for the door.

Once outside, he dodged the glaring beams of the searchlights, pressing himself against the wall. After he got his bearings, he looked toward the fence. Sparks glanced and popped off the metal. Listening to the insect-like buzz, he knew he couldn't clear the electrified fence. His only escape was through the main gate.

He slid along the wall heading in the direction of the gatehouse. After a few yards, he saw the lights of the entrance. By this time a collection of guards had gathered and formed a phalanx, ready to stop anything that came through.

The Phantom estimated he had five shots left, but there were eight armed men. He took aim and squeezed the trigger, dropping one guard. The others scattered like roaches. Some fired wildly into the dark, while others crouched in high alert. The crusader slinked toward a small power transformer. In his mind he could hear the ticking of the timers, and knew he had to get away fast. Although the guards might find *some* of the devices, they would not get them *all*.

He got off another shot and struck a second security guard like a duck in a shooting gallery.

"There he is! I see him!" shouted a voice from the darkness.

The champion waited, fully aware that his pursuers might be engaging in trickery. As a shot rang out, he decided it was time to seek better shelter, but there was none. Bullets popped against the fence. As he watched the sparks, a flash of inspiration came.

It was a roll of the dice, but if he could somehow shutdown the transformer, that might disable the fence. He fired at a switch box then the control panel exploded. The buzzing stopped.

Seeing this as providence, the Phantom started to climb the fence. When he reached the top, he covered the sharp edges with his jacket. Even with the protection of the coat, he ripped a pant cuff before he cleared the barrier. His lungs burned as he ran for his life.

Back in the safety of the woods, first he felt the heat, then the force of the blast lifted him off his feet and he took flight. A tree ended his trip.

The most impressive sight was the orange mushroom cloud. Its pyretic presence stretched far and wide. He'd seen and been the cause of many previous explosions. None were as apocalyptic as this.

• • •

"Pull!" Spano ordered and fired another round. The rifle bucked. His shoulder lurched back from the recoil. The clay pigeon split in two and fell to the earth.

"Pull! Pull!" He gritted his teeth and fired again, obliterating the two decoys. He turned to Olivetti and O'Brien and said, "Good shooting, wouldn't you agree?"

Both men nodded. "You are in rare form, sir," Olivetti praised.

Nicholas Spano put down his gun and brushed off the leather-padded shoulder of his shooting shirt. Pushing the Tyrolian hat up further on his head, he looked O'Brien in the eye.

"Do you know who I visualize when I take aim?"

"No, sir," O'Brien replied.

Spano's nostrils flared. "I see the Phantom Detective! What does that mean to you?" he asked Olivetti.

"It means you're angry over what happened at the Dracon Chemical plant."

The shadowy plutocrat scoffed as he picked up his rifle. "This is not the time for understatement, my smooth friend, but for decisive action. So tell me, what should we do to take care of this monumental problem? Pull!"

Olivetti launched another clay target into the air. Again the pigeon disintegrated and fell to the well-manicured and rich green lawn.

The consultant palmed another pigeon, running his fingers along the smooth edges.

"I suggest we take care of the Phantom once and for all. Kill him."

Spano smiled. "I agree...we are thinking along the same lines."

O'Brien wiped the sweat off his brow as his complexion paled.

Spano looked over at the politician. "What's the matter; you're not going soft on me are you?"

O'Brien swallowed. "I can't stand by and watch any more tragedies! I didn't sign up for this!"

The other men looked at one another and laughed.

"What actually did you think you signed up for?" Spano asked.

O'Brien let out a heavy sigh. "I didn't want anyone to get hurt!"

Spano pointed his gun downward and looked again at Jonny. "He didn't want anybody to get hurt. What do you think about that?"

"I think he better buckle up, because the omelet hasn't been cooked and we have to break a few more eggs."

Olivetti and Spano laughed wickedly.

"Speaking of omelets, how are we coming with our plans for the grand finale?"

"We're right on schedule. The explosion didn't slow us down a bit. We have more than enough contaminant to poison the whole New York City water supply and the surrounding metro area!" Olivetti answered.

"Excellent." Spano chuckled diabolically, turning to O'Brien. "When that last shoe drops, your victory will be imminent. But first, what to do about that annoying fly called the Phantom... Pull!"

With the powerful arm of a baseball player, Olivetti threw another target into the air. Spano took aim and destroyed it.

"I propose we lure him into a trap by going after someone close to him."

"Ah, yes, who might that be? Pull!" Spano demanded. Another clay pigeon soared upward. Spano shot it out of the sky.

"There a few key people he associates with," Olivetti contributed.

"Precisely, but who is the best choice."

• • •

The Phantom, disguised as an everyman, sat on a park bench. Fowler had gotten word to Frank that he wanted to meet with the protector. Uneasy, he surveyed the area. Spano was sure to know that he was the cause of the factory explosion. Retaliation would be his next move. With that in mind, every shadow, every noise was suspect. He flinched slightly when the agent sat down beside him.

"You're not the only one who is stealthy," Fowler laughed.

"I should've seen you coming, I'm slipping."

"You picked a great spot. A good line of sight in all directions."

The disguised crusader nodded in acknowledgment.

Fowler whistled. "I heard you took care of Dracon Chemicals."

The Phantom offered no reply.

"So, what else do you have for me?"

"I have some insight into what they're planning!"

With a grave expression, Dan Fowler turned to the avenger. "I think I do, too, but let's compare notes."

"They're influencing O'Brien's election by committing acts of terror.

Then they'll use those events as a political cudgel to beat Mayor Dewey over the head."

"That makes sense in light of this." Fowler pulled out the city map he stole from the campaign office and gave it to the Phantom. "What do you make of it?"

The Phantom held it up to take advantage of the illumination coming from a streetlamp and studied it. "It looks as if they're setting up medical care stations around the city. This confirms that they're planning something catastrophic!"

"That's what I was thinking as well."

"But *what*?!"

"What indeed," Fowler mused.

"O'Brien contacted Steve Huston and they set up a meeting somewhere downtown. I don't know quite what the main topic will be. My sense tells me he is not completely in support of what Spano is doing. I think if the opportunity arises we might be able to use the information O'Brien provides to our advantage."

The Phantom looked into the distance past the trees. Partially obscured by the vegetation, he saw lights on in the apartment buildings across the street. He pondered how much the city dwellers depended on him to stop this madness.

• • •

Two waitresses rushed back and forth serving customers during the breakfast rush. A short order cook rang a little bell every time an order was ready. Steaming cups of coffee rested in front of weary diners as they buried their noses in the morning edition of *The Clarion*.

Steve Huston sat in a padded burgundy booth and drummed his fingers on the coffee-stained table. He glanced anxiously around the restaurant. When he had talked to O'Brien yesterday, his voice on the phone didn't have its usual dynamic politician tone. He had sounded scared and confused, and his speech was slurred as though he had been drinking. The candidate said he had something to tell him and that it was urgent. To protect himself, O'Brien informed him he would be wearing a disguise so Huston wouldn't see him coming.

After waiting for over an hour, Huston figured O'Brien had gotten cold feet and decided to leave. Huston was only a few feet from the diner when a black Packard pulled up. Two masked men jumped out, whisked him into the backseat, and they sped away.

• • •

"So, what else do you have for me?"

Richard Curtis Van Loan sat in Frank Havens' living room. His face registered a mixture of shock and anger. Why hadn't he seen this one coming?! Huston should have had a back up. Muriel sat by his side on the couch, her hand on his shoulder to calm him. Havens stood by the fireplace, holding the ransom note that had been written on a piece of greasy paper.

"The kidnappers demand that the Phantom Detective is to come alone."

"Are they asking for money?" Muriel inquired.

Havens pulled a wood match from a box on the mantel. He struck it against the marble and pitched it into the fireplace. The wood ignited and crackled. "They want to trade Steve for the Phantom…"

Muriel felt Van Loan's body tense. "Richard, the police and the Phantom will do everything they can to rescue Steve. The best thing you can do is to let them do their job." She was concerned by his angry disposition.

"Where is the meet supposed to take place?" Van Loan asked.

Frank didn't answer as he walked over and picked up the phone.

• • •

Mist hung in the air over the city, making the summer night chilly. With his brim pulled low and his collar turned up, the Phantom Detective stood in the close confines of a phone booth. Any minute the phone would ring. And it did.

The veiled hero picked up the receiver. "Yes?"

"Go to the old Peabody meat packing plant down on the docks. Come alone or the ace cub reporter is dog food," an astral voice ordered.

"How do I know he isn't already dead?" The Phantom heard a click then a dial tone. No one suspicious seemed to be watching, but it was hard to see anything in this obscurity. He would need to be cautious for both his own safety and Huston's.

• • •

The decrepit structure towered over the Phantom Detective. Even though it was a dark night, the crusader could see the decay all around him. Glass from broken windows crunched underfoot. He stepped over twisted metal and rusty pipes. Most of the entrances to the building were boarded up. After diligent searching, he crept down some concrete stairs, squeezed through a tight opening that qualified as the door, and found a way into the basement.

He found the interior of the room dark, damp, and foreboding. Somewhere in a far-off corner a slight but steady drip came from a leaky pipe. The crime fighter, shining a small light, moved gingerly in the blackness. As his eyes adjusted, he could see a spot toward the far end of the room that was a shade lighter than the rest. A passageway?

His foot bumped against a concrete step. Stairs! A railing navigated him upwards. The steps ended at a doorless entryway. Not wanting to alert Houston's captors, he switched off his torch.

As the Phantom Detective passed through the doorway, he saw a naked light bulb casting a dirty yellow glow. He drew his pistol knowing he would soon have company.

As he crept across the floor, he heard the usual sound of clanking pipes and skittering small furry creatures. Although the plant was emptied of furnishings and machinery, the champion still trod carefully. After a few minutes of exploring, he heard a voice. Steve Huston! Finding him couldn't be that easy…and it wasn't.

Venturing down an endless network of corridors and climbing more flights of stairs, the sound of Huston's voice led him into an enormous room. Another glaring light bulb hung above the kidnapped reporter, bound to a wooden chair. Four beefy goons surrounded him. One held a gun to the young ace's head and was probably forcing the lad to call out to the Phantom Detective.

The covert defender spied the scene knowing all along he walked into a trap. But he had to come for Huston and use his wits to get them both out of the dangerous predicament. When he pointed his pistol at the gunmen, all of them laughed.

"You think you have a chance against four of us?"

"Make that five!" Olivetti emerged from a dark corner. With him was Candidate O'Brien, pale and sweating profusely.

The Phantom held his gun steady. "I'm the one you really want! Let Huston go!"

The slimy counselor stepped into the middle of the room to take center stage, signifying that he was running the show. "Right now, we have the upper hand. Drop your weapon or the scribe's brains are splattered all over the floor."

The Phantom noticed the politician's uneasy demeanor and decided to take a gamble. "Your mayoral candidate doesn't seem to be all that well. Could it be he isn't completely in step with your plans?"

Olivetti scowled and regarded O'Brien. "Never mind him. Drop the gun!"

The vigilante refused to budge. Olivetti looked furtively at his henchmen. They were fully aware of the stalemate that was taking place. The

Phantom noticed Olivetti ever so slightly start to shake. The masked man then pointed the gun at O'Brien.

"You know…if I shoot your wunderkind candidate that would make all of this irrelevant."

A look of shock washed over Olivetti's face, but he shook it off.

"You wouldn't do that! Besides we can always find a replacement," Olivetti retorted.

The masked investigator laughed. "There won't be enough time to groom anyone else. O'Brien's demise would throw all of your plans into turmoil. Let Huston go or I shoot the grandstander."

His remark had the effect he was hoping for; to corner Olivetti. With seething rage, the advisor turned again to his men. "Get him, you fools! Bring him to me so I can inflict maximum pain."

The four men rushed the hero. The Phantom backed into the doorway and expertly met the challenge. Not wanting to endanger Huston's life, he secured his weapon and greeted the first goon head-on with a punch to his left eye. Then he grabbed his shirt collar, spun, and tossed him down the stairwell. The large man's flabby physique did little to soften fall.

As the other three lined up, the Phantom focused on the next one. His challenger proved to be more artful with his fists and threw a succession of fast punches that caught the cloaked sleuth in the face and he stumbled forward. The other two assailants attempted to box him in, but the Phantom pivoted, pulling his initial challenger away from the other attackers. The crime fighter jumped and delivered a direct blow to the man's knee cap, shattering it. He howled in pain and fell to the floor.

His remaining foes drew their weapons in frustration. The Phantom, as quick as a gunslinger, drew his pistol, dropped to one knee, and plugged both adversaries. His hope was not to kill anyone else, but there was no other choice. He turned his gun on Olivetti, who now had O'Brien in a stranglehold and a pistol trained on Huston.

"I don't suppose we can resolve this peacefully, can we?"

Olivetti spat and snarled like a wounded honey badger. He looked at the hero with burning eyes. "End of the line, you masked nuisance! This is the last time I'll say it, drop the gun or I kill them both."

The conversation ended with one shot fired followed by one crimson bloom on Olivetti's face. He let go of O'Brien, mouthed a silent tortured plea, and spiraled to the floor.

The cloaked crusader turned to see Dan Fowler emerge from a dark corner. The G-Man smiled, holding his smoking gun.

"Sorry, Phantom, but Washington isn't about to let you take all the credit for saving New York City!"

"Oh, yes, New York City, any ideas?"

Both Fowler and the Phantom untied Steve Huston. Then they used those binds to secure O'Brien to the man with the injured leg.

"We'll leave these guys for the blue coats," said the Phantom Detective.

"Sorry I caused so much trouble, fellas!" the reporter chimed in.

"You were deceived. It could've happened to anyone, possibly even us!" Fowler replied.

The avenger kneeled next to Robert O'Brien. "You apparently have had a change of heart. Do the right thing and tell us what they're planning."

Robert O'Brien looked at the two like he was in a living nightmare and said nothing.

Fowler crouched down and grabbed his shirt. "People's lives are at stake. So it's important, son, that you tell us what you know. I need the time, place, and what they're planning. If you fail to cooperate, I will resort to other means of persuasion."

The Phantom glared through his domino mask at the frightened man. "I'll be more than happy to help with that persuasion."

Fowler grabbed O'Brien's hair and started to pull his head back.

The man blubbered, "Okay, okay, they're going to poison Indian Reservoir upstate."

"That supplies all of New York City! Who?" the Phantom demanded.

"Spano and Olivetti. They wanted me to be the savior, swoop in with medical aid, and look good for the press! It was the only way to defeat Dewey. But I never wanted it to come to this!"

"Well, it did, and now you must be brought to justice. Steve and I will wait for the authorities. Phantom, I suggest you head up to Indian Reservoir. I will be there as fast as I can!"

The Phantom Detective nodded and turned to leave.

"Hey, Phantom!" Huston yelled.

The hero turned to the reporter.

"Thanks!"

"It's my job," the Phantom replied as he slipped into the darkness.

• • •

Lunar light shimmered on the big lake surrounded by dense forest. Except for a government structure on the north shore, the area was uninhabited. Other than one paved road that dead-ended at a barbed wire fence and gate, logging trails were the only access to the reservoir.

The Phantom had driven up to the entrance and found it compromised. They were already here poisoning the water!

Wasting no time, he barreled through the ruined gate. It didn't take long before his headlights shone upon a tanker truck backed up to the water's edge. That tanker must contain the toxic compound! Three men protected by black rubber suits were connecting a heavy hose to the truck. Realizing he had arrived in time gave the savior hope, but it was short-lived. Bullets began shattering his windows. The Detective grabbed his machine gun from the passenger seat and jumped out of the moving car as it veered off toward the lake. More bullets perforated the automobile and it exploded, lifting it off the ground. Every one ducked for cover.

The Phantom peered out from behind a log. A flying bullet ricocheted near his head, sending sawdust into his face. He hit the dirt. More bullets whistled overhead. The avenging angel lifted his gun and fired a short burst. The shooting stopped momentarily. Taking advantage of the pause, he popped up to get a bead on those hunting him. He saw one assailant poke his head out around a corner of the government building. With one well-placed shot, the Phantom tagged him.

This caused a volley of rounds. The veiled protector ducked again. When it grew quiet he looked up and discovered his foes were attempting to flank his position. Crouching, he fired at those approaching from the right and made his way to the structure. His ploy had caused all of them to seek their own cover. The Phantom used this reprieve to make a dash for better shelter.

He craned from behind a government truck. The color of his trench coat allowed him to blend in with the gray vehicle. Because of his concealment, his pursuers made the mistake of giving up their position. The Phantom picked them off as if they were beer cans on a fence.

Now that they were out of the way, he must get to the tanker. With a short sprint, he reached the truck and saw the three men were again lugging the hose to the lake. As he began to run toward them, he was tripped from behind. Nicolas Spano!

Spano was quick to smack the vigilante's gun hand. The polished mahogany cane sent radial pain through the Phantom's arm, causing a spasm. He released his gun. The shadowy rich man whacked him on the shoulder, inflicting more torment on the Phantom.

With a flick of his cane, Spano unsheathed a serrated sword. Expert fencing skill enabled him to go after the crime fighter like a butcher carving meat. The Phantom dodged most of the jabs and thrusts, but two sliced his cheek. From his position on the ground, he kicked upward at the man's knee. The blow did not deter the billionaire. As he was about to pierce the cloaked crusader's heart, a shot rang out. Spano coughed as blood dribbled out of his mouth. His sword felt to the ground as he clutched his gut. Once again Dan Fowler had saved the Phantom.

By this time the three men were along the shoreline and had placed the hose in the water. Adrenaline and a sense of urgency coursed through the crusader's body. With their guns blazing, he and Fowler rushed the trio. All three convulsed when the gunfire riddled their bodies.

The G-Man was the first to arrive at the edge of the lake. He wrestled the hose out of the water. The Phantom reached the truck and pulled the lever, stopping the flow of poison. In the distance, police sirens wailed and flashing beacons washed the woods in a bloody radiance. The glaring flashlight of a uniformed cop spotlighted the two.

The Phantom looked out over the reservoir, then at the officer. "Tell your supervisor to get the water commissioner on the phone, now!"

• • •

Richard Curtis Van Loan drank from a tall sweating glass of lemonade. When he finished, Muriel poured him another. She poured one for herself and for her father, too.

"This is good lemonade, Honey!" Van Loan said.

"You better believe it! It's freshly squeezed by hand."

Frank Havens raised his glass to his daughter. "As always, dear, everything you do is done with great care."

Van Loan nodded in agreement.

Muriel blushed but remained salty. She looked over at her beau and shook her head. "Father tells me that the Phantom Detective helped Agent Fowler foil a sinister plot to destroy New York City."

"Really?" Van Loan asked. "The citizens will never know."

"No need to panic or upset them more than they already are. They are still reeling from the news that O'Brien was arrested for check fraud and is going to jail," Havens added.

Muriel clucked her tongue. "A nice little cover story that Fowler concocted and Steve Huston reported."

"Nice indeed."

Richard Curtis Van Loan stared out at the vast lawn and the murky water of Long Island Sound, wondering what his next caper would be. He was ready to answer the call and hoped it would be soon. Muriel waved her hand in front of his face and snapped him out of his daydream.

"Stay with us, chief. Not sure where you went this time, but someday maybe you can take me with you," Muriel said.

Van Loan smiled. "Sorry, I was lost in thought again."

Muriel eyed him suspiciously as she looked at the wounds on his face. "You know, buster, I'm still having a hard time believing you got those nasty cuts from playing polo. Especially since I know you didn't have a game scheduled last night. Want to fess up to something?"

Van Loan's eyes went wide as he shot Havens a desperate look.

THE END

The Politics of Personal Destruction

I have been a fan of Airship 27 for about a decade. So I was more than thrilled when Ron asked me to jump aboard "The Airship" and write a story. I chose the Phantom Detective because I liked the fact that his uniform was a fedora and trench coat over say, tights. I also like that he was a prototype for Batman right down to a beacon summoning him to action. His ability as a master of disguise was intriguing to me, as well as his double-identity, a wealthy lothario by day and masked hero by night.

As I thought about and started to map out the story, it became clearer and clearer this was to be a buddy tale. Who better to assist the Phantom in fighting crime than Dan Fowler G-Man, since they had joined forces in the past? The Phantom and Dan had compatible methods of fighting crime.

The story had to be new pulp which I found to be a challenge. It was important to keep things current and relevant to readers, but at the same time maintain the flavor of the original pulp stories. I tend to lean more toward the retro side of things so I had to find an angle that was fresh.

The politics of personal destruction is when a politician goes to great lengths to demonize their opponent through personal attack ads and other dirty tricks. This being the world of pulp, why not take it one step further and have a villain who is bent on destroying New York City in order to get a puppet-like mayoral candidate elected; thus the title, "The Campaign of Destruction."

This premise is in one instance absurd, and in the other, quite topical. We are living in the golden age of terrorism and have arch villains even worse than Nicholas Spano perpetrating heinous acts. Readers can relate to the horror of bombings and use of poison like anthrax but I thought it was appropriate to make the acts of terror a bit on the ridiculous side to stay within the realm of pulp – the bomb which unleashes Hydra is a good example. Maybe I was channeling a 1960s Batman episode.

The Phantom Detective is perfect for this type of scenario. In his universe, the opinion of him and his crusade against crime is divided into two camps. To some he is a hero, and to others he is a terrorist in his own right. So who better to fight terrorism than a perceived terrorist?

In a piece like this, you do not have time to add a lot of narration about character and feelings, an aspect which complements my writing style. Characters in the world of pulp are defined by their actions. In the case of the Phantom Detective, his actions define him as a hero and set him apart from those he is fighting against. The story was a pleasure to write.

• • •

WHIT HOWLAND - made his authorial debut in 2010 when his first story *Huey Dusk* was published. Huey Dusk, a private eye clown, is modeled after Mickey Spillane's Mike Hammer. In this world, clowns and mimes are a species and not humans pretending to be clowns or mimes. It is a dark and absurd world about tough characters championing good causes, which happen to fall in line with their own interests. Three subsequent stories about Huey Dusk have been published. All can be found at www.untreedreads.com.

A Johnny Nickle story penned by Whit for Pro Se Press's Charles Beckman Presents line will soon to be released.

Future writing plans include another Huey Dusk caper, a western, a spinoff from the Johnny Nickle tale, and many more pulp adventures.

Whit resides in Godfrey, Illinois with his wife and three cats and divides his time between writing and volunteering at the local public library. In his free time, he reads lots and lots of pulp and crime fiction, writes poetry, and serves on his church board.

Harbor Lights
by Robert M. Ricci

August 1937

Richard Curtis Van Loan had an extra spark to his walk this warm and hazy evening. The Manhattan skyline revealed sparkling stars as he exited from the swanky hotel. He had just ended a marvelous evening with his latest romantic flame, stunning Broadway starlet, Miriam Hayden.

He suppressed a grin as he fondly recalled the daring neckline of her shimmering cocktail dress. It had accented her flaming red hair nicely, so much so that the waiter had carelessly spilled a tray of drinks, straining for a better view.

Van Loan's reverie was interrupted by a sharp jab at the back of his rib cage. He knew instantly it was the tip of a gun pressed against his body. His muscles tightened, ready for action.

"Don't think about being a hero, rich guy! This will all end better if you just listen to me."

The voice was gruff and daunting, a seasoned thug.

Van Loan was furious with himself. He couldn't believe he had let a common mugger get the drop on him!

"Listen, pal, don't do something you will regret."

His tone was stern but not hostile. He didn't want the thug to get an itchy finger before he could react.

"Any regrets will be yours!" the creep snarled. "I just want your cash, rich guy!"

Van Loan wasn't at all surprised that he had been pointed out as a wealthy target. His picture had been plastered on the cover of the Clarion at least three times this summer alone. The playboy was usually on-guard for such encounters, but his attention had been squarely focused on the memories of Miriam Hayden's supple bosom. It was his only character flaw, his overzealous attraction to beautiful women.

"Okay," Van Loan instructed in a slow, deliberate voice. "My wallet is inside my back pocket. Let me get it for you."

He began to reach behind his back, but the mugger thrust the revolver harder into his side.

"No sudden moves, rich guy! I'll just help myself to it if you don't mind."

114

Van Loan felt a grubby hand claw at his trouser pocket, before it reeled in its prize.

"Okay, "Van Loan stated. "You have my money. Now go. I haven't seen you, and I won't report this to the police."

There was a moment of silence before the deep throated mugger responded.

"I'm not finished with you yet, rich guy. Turn around real nice and slow."

Van Loan did as he was instructed. He turned to view a weasel faced man with crooked teeth and a scruffy chin. The mugger glared at him in the bright moonlight.

"What are you staring at, rich guy? Think you're better than me because of those fancy duds you got on?"

Van Loan shook his head.

"I don't think I'm better than you, just more fortunate, pal. You have my wallet. This doesn't have to get hostile."

The creep snarled at him.

"I said I wasn't through with you."

Van Loan was starting to lose patience. He was already angry with himself for letting a common thief get the drop on him. He tried to maintain his composure.

"Listen to me." Van Loan began. "I know times are tough and work is hard to come by, but sooner or later you will get caught and prison life is no picnic."

The mugger growled.

"Shut your mouth, rich guy." He eyed Van Loan from top to bottom. His gaze stuck on Richard's expensive wrist watch.

Van Loan noticed the thug's desire.

"My watch? You want it? It's yours if you just take it and go."

The thief didn't care for Van Loan's paternal voice.

"Don't get smart on me, rich guy. I'll decide what I take. And it may be your life!"

That did it for Richard Curtis Van Loan.

"You want this watch? Now?"

The mugger nodded greedily.

"Give it to me!"

"Here you go then."

Van Loan exploded in a frenzy of action. With blinding speed, his left arm chopped down on the mugger's wrist, breaking bones. Simultaneously, his right fist shot forward and clipped the creep on the jaw. The mugger dropped like a sack of bricks. His eyes rolled into the back of his head before he lost consciousness.

"I'm sorry," Van Loan muttered sarcastically, "did you mean I was supposed to take it off first? My wrong."

He received no response. The thug was out cold on the sidewalk as a crowd started to gather. He could hear rumbles of recognition. Van Loan, usually not shy for the spotlight, was in no mood for publicity this evening.

He bent over and retrieved his wallet. After a brief hesitation, he withdrew a twenty dollar bill and shoved it into the mugger's front pocket.

"Just on the off chance that you really are down on your luck." He whispered.

The crowd began surging closer to Van Loan, hoping for a better look at the millionaire playboy.

"Did you see that?" a middle aged man proclaimed. "One punch! Van Loan hits harder than Joe Louis!"

Van Loan didn't relish the comparison. He desired to maintain a casual profile as a laid back playboy, a direct contradiction of his true character, because behind that image of a wealthy socialite, hid the true nature of Richard Curtis Van Loan.

Startled gasps emitted from a throng across the street. Van Loan began to walk over and apologize and assure them the situation was safe, when he noticed their gaze wasn't focused on him at all. The concerned citizens were looking up at the sky, specifically to the top of the Clarion Building, home of Manhattan's bestselling newspaper.

"Do you see it?"

"Is it true what that means?"

The "it" the crowd was referring to was a bright red beacon flashing atop the roof of the mammoth building.

Van Loan let out a sigh. He had been hoping for an early evening of rest and a good book. Instead, his evening had just become unpredictable.

The red light being emitted from the beacon above the Clarion was a signal meant to summon Manhattan's greatest crime fighter, the Phantom Detective.

"They say criminals lock their doors when that light flashes!" one gentleman shouted above the din.

Richard Curtis Van Loan certainly hoped the stranger was correct, for he had a personal stake in the outcome. You see, Van Loan was the Phantom Detective!

• • •

Frank Havens paced nervously back and forth on the graveled roof of the Clarion Building. He wrung the sweat from his shirt as he circled the area like a predatory shark. The gruff publisher of the Clarion usually had a scarlet face from barking orders under the intense pressure of his job, but tonight his pallor was as pale as the moon.

"You summoned me?"

Frank Havens turned in the direction of the unearthly voice. He had no idea of the Phantom Detective's true identity. In fact, he would be shocked if he knew it was his daughter Muriel's friend, Richard, shielding his face with a domino mask. The Phantom wore a dark overcoat and black fedora.

"Phantom, thank you for coming."

Van Loan had trained his vocals to project a deeper timber to his voice when assuming the Phantom guise. The results were chillingly unnatural. You couldn't tell what direction the voice was coming from.

"Frank Havens, I have pledged my aid to you and the citizens of Manhattan. Tell me how I can be of assistance."

Havens shoulders slumped. He began to speak, but the words caught in his throat. All he could mutter was one word.

"Muriel."

Muriel Havens was the publisher's beautiful raven haired daughter and sometimes beau of socialite Richard Curtis Van Loan.

The Phantom caught himself trembling. He steeled himself for whatever horror awaited. He could tell the news was grave. Frank Havens did not take the responsibility of the beacon lightly. He only used it for situations beyond the control of ordinary law enforcement.

"What is wrong sir?" Van Loan demanded, trying to instill some strength into the weary publisher.

Havens cupped a hand over his mouth, almost as if to keep the words from spilling out. Finally, he was able to release a statement.

"It's Muriel. Something has happened!"

Van Loan felt his heart leap into his throat.

"Your daughter, sir?"

Havens nodded.

"Is she?" Van Loan began.

Havens shrugged.

"I don't know. I don't know what happened."

Van Loan tried to calm him down.

"Start at the beginning, sir. It's important you gather your composure."

Havens released a sarcastic chuckle.

"Easy for you to say. You don't know her. That's my baby girl!"

Van Loan wanted to scream. He wanted to tell him that Muriel meant the world to him also, but his role as the Phantom prevented him from doing so.

"I'm here to help, Mr. Havens. Start from the beginning, and give me the details."

Frank Havens wiped a bead of perspiration from his eyelids. The muggy August heat was overwhelming and the excess weight he carried from eating unhealthy treats was taking its toll on his middle aged frame.

"My Muriel, she's a feisty one." Havens began. "Always trying to prove to me that she is a real reporter and not just the publisher's daughter."

Van Loan fought back a grin. He knew Muriel Havens well. She had earned her position on the paper, no doubt about it.

"Is she working on a story for you?" the Phantom inquired.

Havens nodded, his white shirt streaked with newspaper ink and sweat.

"She was on to something big, my Muriel. But she is a secretive one. Show me a reporter who isn't. Anyway, she told me she had a tip, a good one. Explosive, she called it."

The Phantom nodded, encouraging the publisher to continue. The big man seemed to grow calmer as he recalled details. His newspaper background was starting to kick in.

"Naturally, all cub reporters think they're working on the mother of all stories, but this time Muriel was sure of it. She said she had to get out to New England immediately."

The Phantom intervened.

"Where exactly?"

Havens shrugged. "Couldn't tell you. She was taking a train to Boston."

"Was she alone, sir?"

Havens emitted a slight guffaw.

"You think I'd send my baby girl on the road alone?"

The Phantom remained stolid.

"Anyway," Havens continued, "After arguing with her to no avail, I knew she was going to head up there anyway, so I financed it under the agreement that she would not be alone."

"Who did you send with her?"

Havens folded his arms, the nerves having relaxed a bit more.

"Steve Huston."

The Phantom nodded. "A good reporter, and a good man."

Havens agreed. "I know. I keep telling Muriel she should settle down with him instead of waiting for that lazy playboy Van Loan to marry her. Believe me; those types are not the settling down type."

The Phantom was taken aback by the rejection.

"My sources in law enforcement tell me Richard Curtis Van Loan is an upstanding citizen and a valuable member of our society."

Havens waved his hands, sheepishly.

"I know, I know! Honestly, he's a fine man. It's just that Muriel is my baby, and no father wants to see his daughter pine for a love that can't be returned."

"Does she love him?" Phantom wondered.

A curious scowl appeared on Haven's face. That was a reflection of his reporter background. He stared at the Phantom curiously.

"Why do you care?"

Phantom was taken aback. He scrambled for a way to deflect the attention.

"Just making sure I get all the facts, Mr. Havens. Even a minute detail could make the difference in a life or death situation."

Satisfied with the response, Frank Havens continued his tale.

"Anyway, she and Huston left New York five days ago. They were going to check into the Hotel Manger in Boston, but when I called the hotel, the concierge told me she hadn't checked in."

"Maybe they found another hotel?" Phantom offered.

Havens shook his head.

"No, reporters always let the paper know where they are. That way we can get information to them. I'm telling you something is wrong!"

Phantom took a moment to reflect. As Van Loan, he wanted to unleash a barrage of questions at the seasoned publisher, but his role as crime fighter forced him to stick to the details.

"Huston is a fine man. I've had encounters with him in the past. He can handle himself in a jam."

Havens agreed. "Steve's a tough guy, that's for sure. If he ever gets tired of writing, he could have a career in the ring."

Phantom changed the subject.

"Have you contacted the Boston authorities?"

All the color drained from Frank Haven's face again, as if he recalled a horrible incident. He fished in his pocket and pulled out a crumpled piece of paper.

"This is why I set off the beacon, Phantom."

"What is it?"

Havens unfurled the paper. His hand was trembling when he passed it over to the Phantom.

"My secretary got the call this evening. She knew the message was important, so they tracked me down in Times Square."

Phantom stared at the paper. There were three words scrawled on it.

"You did the right thing, Mr. Havens."

Frank Havens nodded, a lump in his throat.

"She's all I have Phantom. Will you help?"

The Phantom Detective laid a sturdy hand on the publisher's shoulder.

"I won't rest until she's returned to you sir."

He stared at the paper again. In deep black marker, the secretary had copied down the words she the menacing voice had uttered.

Don't call police!

• • •

After a few more minutes of intense questioning, The Phantom agreed to investigate the case of the missing journalist. Without waiting for a goodbye, he withdrew his grapple hook and descended from the rooftop much to Frank Haven's surprise. The Clarion was practically a skyscraper. No ordinary man could make that descent, but then again, there was nothing ordinary about the Phantom Detective.

The Phantom actually only descended a few stories before pushing his way into one of the open editorial windows, mostly deserted at this hour of the night. Removing his coat and fedora, he instantly transformed back into Richard Curtis Van Loan, suave millionaire playboy.

Van Loan appreciated the fact that the offices were vacant. He was able to plop himself down into a private corner office to use one of the phones. His fingers snapped the rotary dials at blazing speed. He was calling a familiar number.

The voice on the other line was sleepy, it's owner awakened from a pleasant slumber.

"This better be good, and if it's you Murphy, I'll have your money on Friday."

Van Loan stifled a laugh.

"Lost another wager, I'd bet?"

Jerry Lannigan straightened at attention, reflexively issuing a salute. He was dressed only in a pair of boxers, the sweltering heat hindering his sleep. Embarrassed, he dropped his hand sheepishly, glad no one had witnessed his folly.

"That you Dick, old chum? Or do you go by Richard now that you made some coin?"

Van Loan was joyous to hear his old buddy's voice. The pair had served together in the military, and had flown dozens of hazardous missions which led to an unbreakable bond between the men. This didn't prevent them from razzing each other.

"I know you're alone, Jerry. There isn't a woman who would fall for your idea of romance. Still stealing flowers from grave yards?"

Lannigan snorted on the other end.

"That was a long time ago, and they were for my mother! Besides, if my employer paid better wages, I'd be able to find a wife and settle down."

Lannigan was referring to Van Loan. The man was employed part time as a pilot and engineer for the millionaire.

"Don't give me that sad tale, Jerry. You know I don't fly as much as I'd like to with all this paperwork I'm forced to deal with, and my offer still stands."

"There you go again. You know I can't do that routine! Eight hours behind a desk listening to blowhards, and wearing a tie! No, sir, that ain't the life I signed up for."

Van Loan agreed.

"Okay, Jerry, listen up. I know it's the middle of the night, but I got a hot potato."

Lannigan's ears perked up.

"Big business deal, boss? "

Van Loan couldn't hide his lament.

"I wish, Jerry. Personal emergency." He didn't feel like filling in his employee with the details. "I need to get to Boston right away."

Lannigan waited patiently.

"I need my plane."

"Boss, I don't mean to sound rude, but you got a lot of planes! You want me to fly you up to Beantown?"

Van Loan shook his head.

"Solo mission, buddy. Sorry."

Lannigan licked his chops.

"You ain't cutting me out of some action, are you boss? Or, wait a minute, you sly dog! It's a woman! Isn't it?"

Van Loan croaked his reply.

"Yes."

"I knew it!"

You could hear the spunk in Jerry Lannigan's voice.

"Not what you think, pal"

Lannigan would have none of it.

"Sure, boss. Should I load a crate of champagne on for you? Maybe some cans of caviar?"

Van Loan grew impatient.

"Jerry, stop your babbling and listen. I need a plane, the plane."

Lannigan emitted a slow whistle. It reverberated into his small desk fan, the only relief from the scorching heat.

"You serious, boss?"

Van Loan replied in a stoic tone.

"Never been more serious."

Lannigan sighed and searched around for his trousers. It didn't take long. His room consisted of a cot, a wobbly wooden chair and an empty cupboard.

"The plane it is." He jumped into the wrinkled trousers and grabbed a shirt from the pile on the floor. "I take it you mean right now?"

Van Loan dismissed his friend's uppity tone.

"I've already sent a car to take you to the hangar."

The hangar was Van Loan's private one on Long Island. That is where he kept the plane. Lannigan couldn't help but whistle again.

"I sure hope this dame appreciates it. That plane is one of a kind."

Van Loan looked at his wrist watch, remembering the earlier incident. He knew the Phantom would never be caught off-guard like his more casual alter ego.

"Have her ready, Jerry."

Lannigan hung up. He could hear the roar of a Rolls Royce pulling up to his apartment building.

"Damn, Dick, you sent the best! Boy, the neighbors will be jealous. Wish I had time to dress up better. Oh, well, no fuss."

He didn't bother to lock his door. Why worry about it? There wasn't anything worth taking. He hurried down the stairway two at a time. The driver was waiting with the car door open.

"Mister Lannigan."

Jerry chuckled at the formal tone.

"Could you say it a little louder? I want these folks to know I hob knob with the big shots."

The driver remained stone faced.

"Where to, Mister Lannigan?"

He managed a slight emphasis on the title this time, much to Jerry's delight.

"Take me to her, Jeeves. The big man wants his baby."

The driver allowed his lips to curl ever so slightly.

The "her" they were referring to was the pride of Van Loan's small fleet, his brand new Bugatti, series 100P, arguably the fastest plane in the world. It had been known to reach speeds in excess of 500 mph. Van Loan had commissioned a custom model painted Royal Blue.

The only other Bugatti in New York belonged to a well-known scientific adventurer who dwelled on the 86th floor of a Manhattan skyscraper.

Lannigan's excitement rose as he continued to get closer to the airstrip.

"She's a real beauty! Twin engines, counter rotating propellers, yes, sir, the boss really bought himself one impressive piece of machinery."

The driver cleared his throat and pointed to the initials on the steering wheel. Lannigan snarled.

"Don't get angry on me, bud! I wasn't downplaying the Rolls at all. It's just, the Bugatti. She's in a class all by herself!"

The driver sighed and kept on driving. He knew a man like Jerry Lannigan would rather die than admit any machine could rival the invention of the modern airplane.

• • •

Richard Curtis Van Loan had packed only one long bag of clothing and a small briefcase. The briefcase contained his Phantom gear, costume, mask, make-up kit and forensic tools. The Bugatti was sleek, but not roomy.

When he arrived at the Long Island hangar, the place was deserted. Fortunately, his men had left the gate unlocked and swiveled open. He was able to drive right up to the well-lit hangar. He could hear Jerry Lannigan whistling at a frenzied pace.

"Dick!" Lannigan came rushing toward him. He had donned a pair of aviator togs. He pointed at his wardrobe. "Just in case you came to your senses and wanted a real pilot to drive you!"

Van Loan grinned and feigned a jab at his maniacal friend.

"Don't be like that Jerry! I bet you've driven this doll at least twice as many times as I have!"

Lannigan nodded. "True, enough."

Van Loan rubbed a finger across the gleaming surface of his airship. As he expected, not a speck of dust or grime.

"I see you've prepped her."

Lannigan waved at the Bugatti proudly.

"All gassed up and ready to fly. Beantown will be in for a sight when you land this beauty."

Van Loan agreed. "For sure."

"Speaking of landing," asked Lannigan, "Do you want me to call ahead and arrange for a car to be waiting at Boston Airport?"

Van Loan shook his head.

"Already taken care of. I called an old friend from Harvard to pick me up." He laughed. "Actually, he's not that old. Still taking classes."

Lannigan shrugged.

"Anyone I might know?"

Van Loan pursed his lips.

"Doubtful, but the kid has a presence about him that is undeniable. I have a feeling he'll make his mark on the world."

Lannigan was interested.

'That so? What's this chaps name, boss?"

Van Loan cleared his throat.

"Young Jack Kennedy."

• • •

John Kennedy was all of twenty years old. Van Loan had known him since he was a boy. The wavy haired youth exuded charisma.

"Mr. Van Loan, a pleasure!" young Kennedy greeted him with a firm handshake.

Van Loan whistled his appreciation. "Easy, son. I'm not one of those farm hands you had to impress."

Kennedy grinned. "You heard? Pops said no son of his was going to grow up without some adversity. He shipped me off to Arizona last summer to work as a ranch hand."

Van Load gripped the youth's firm biceps.

"I'd say it worked out for everyone except Yale. I wouldn't want to go up against you in a game of pigskin."

Van Loan was referring to American Football.

Kennedy shook his head.

"I do love my football, not to mention a round of golf, but my true passion is the water. We Kennedys love the ocean. I'm hoping to make the Harvard swim team."

"All gassed up and ready to fly."

"You will John, and stop calling me Mr. Van Loan. I'm no senior citizen. Call me Richard."

Kennedy slapped him on the back.

"That is some fancy wings you flew in on."

Van Loan smiled back at the Bugatti.

"What good is money if you can't spoil yourself once in a while?"

They both had a good laugh and Kennedy helped carry Van Loan's baggage. It was early dawn and Boston Airport wasn't that active. Van Loan swiped some sweat from his brow. The humidity had followed him from New York.

"Can't wait to get out of these duds and take a cold shower." He mentioned.

Kennedy smiled, flashing his wide choppers.

"Plenty of time for that, Richard."

"Is the hotel far?"

"Not at all, but we have to make a stop first."

Van Loan stiffened. He didn't want to alert his companion to the dire straits Muriel Havens might be involved with. Kennedy continued to flash his brilliant smile.

"You're my host." Van Loan conceded.

Kennedy motioned to a vehicle. Much to Van Loan's surprise, it was a clunker. Kennedy spotted his apprehension.

"Don't let her fool you, Richard. That girl has a lot of tread on those tires, but she hasn't let me down yet, besides I didn't want to risk my new car through the Sumner."

Van Loan arched an eyebrow. "Beg your pardon?"

"The Sumner. It's the tunnel connecting the airport to East Boston. They just finished it a couple of years ago. It goes right underneath the Boston Harbor. Can you imagine that?"

Van Loan gulped. "Lucky me."

Kennedy slapped a firm hand on Van Loan's shoulder.

"Don't turn yellow on me. Anyone that can fly that whatchamacallit, should be able to travel an underground tunnel without blinking an eye."

Van Loan laughed.

"Can't argue with that, Jack. If you don't mind me asking, why are we going to East Boston?"

Kennedy's eyes widened. "Are you daft? You New Yorkers really do think you live in the center of the universe. Don't you read the sheets?"

Van Loan shrugged. "I check the stocks religiously."

Kennedy laughed. "You and Pops both. But don't you look at the good stuff?" When Van Loan didn't answer, a scowl formed on Kennedy's face. "C'mon, Van Loan, what day is it?"

"August 9th, why?"

Kennedy slapped his forehead.

"History might be made today. You picked the perfect day to come to Boston, my friend!"

Van Loan showed no sign of recognition.

Kennedy spilled the beans.

"Seabiscuit is racing here today!"

• • •

Kennedy took his time travelling through the darkened Sumner tunnel. The cavernous underground way had opened in 1934 to much trepidation. Scientists warned there was no way to really measure the pressure of the sea waves battering the reinforced walls. Many Bostonians refused to drive through it. Jack Kennedy wasn't one of them. He thrived on adventure.

"Isn't this a hoot?" he hollered.

Van Loan didn't open his mouth. The tunnel was not well ventilated and the musty air combined with the sweltering heat was making the air fetid. On top of that, he was running on an empty stomach. He felt like he was going to dry heave.

Kennedy glanced over at his passenger.

"Don't make me tell Pops you couldn't handle this. You know how he plays up a rivalry."

Van Loan nodded, trying to conserve oxygen.

"Joe is a good man. You should be proud."

"I am. Everything, I am, I owe to my Pops."

At last Van Loan glimpsed daylight. He knew the terror had come to an end.

Kennedy almost seemed disappointed.

"East Boston means a lot to my family, Richard. Pops was born here, right over on Meridian Street. He told me never to forget my roots or the people."

Van Loan was feeling better now that he could suck in mouthfuls of fresh air.

"Good advice, Jack."

The drive to Suffolk Downs did not take long. Opening shortly after the creation of the Sumner Tunnel, the race track had enjoyed moderate success in its infancy. Today would prove to be a measuring stick. Kennedy predicted record breaking crowds to descend upon East Boston to get a glimpse of the horse who had inspired so many Americans.

"The race is called the Massachusetts Handicap, Richard. The purse is gigantic; I think well in excess of fifty thousand dollars."

Van Loan whistled.

"That's a lot of money to see animals race around an oval."

Kennedy flashed his choppers again.

"Animals? Seabiscuit is more of a symbol than anything, Richard. He appeals to the everyday American, proof that hard work and a lot of patience can be rewarded with unlimited success."

Van Loan wrinkled his brow. "I don't follow."

Kennedy chuckled. "He represents the American dream, my friend. You see he wasn't always a champion. Lost more than his share of races when he first broke out on the scene, but Tom Smith, the trainer, saw something in that horse that no one else had glimpsed. He encouraged his boss, Charles Howard to buy Seabiscuit. You know what they paid?"

Van Loan shook his head.

"A mere eight thousand dollars!" Kennedy blurted. "For the greatest horse in racing history."

Van Loan was starting to feel a vibe from Kennedy. The kid was a natural salesman. His energy was overwhelming. One couldn't help but feed off it. It was hard to believe he was only twenty years old.

"How long you been following the ponies?" Van Loan inquired.

Kennedy shrieked. "I don't. I follow the people, my friend, and right now the people are glued to that horse. I'll tell you, it's no secret why he is here today. Pops and a lot of other power brokers made this happen. This event will put that race track on the map, and Boston will have another feather in its cap."

"So this is about politics?"

Again, the youth flashed his wide smile. "Isn't everything?"

• • •

The Massachusetts Handicap proved to be anticlimactic. To say that Seabiscuit won the race convincingly would be an understatement. The mighty stallion, had indeed trounced his opponents. In doing so, he shattered not only the Suffolk Downs speed record, but had also captured his largest purse to date.

Young Jack Kennedy was ecstatic. He used the spotlight to press flesh and renew friendships. Van Loan realized now why the entrepreneur was so eager to attend the race that day. He was in full political mode, selling himself as a future candidate. Despite his baby-face and lack of experience, the wealthy clientele flocked to Kennedy like he was a messiah. Van Loan was impressed.

"You really now how to hold fort." He commented to the wavy haired youth as they headed out of the parking lot and back toward the down-town area.

Kennedy flashed his patented "aw shucks" look, but Van Loan wasn't buying.

"Your daddy has huge aspirations for you, son. I think his faith will be rewarded."

"Thank you, Mr. Van Loan. I appreciate your confidence, but I must profess that I'm my own man. Pops might have molded me and pointed me in certain directions, but the choices I make will be my own. This country has just gone through a real rough stretch, and for a while things didn't look bright, but I see recovery taking place every day. Just look at what I've shown you today. A brand new tunnel that generated income and jobs for thousands and a successful race track that proves Americans have a few extra bucks in their wallets again. I couldn't be more proud to be a citizen of this country."

Van Loan stared at the youth's face. He could see genuine honesty in those chiseled features. This young man believed what he preached. If he was a symbol of the youth movement in America, the country was in good hands.

"I had a wonderful time, Jack, but I am here on business. I really appreciate you shuttling me around town."

"Least I could do for a friend of the family. Just be aware, someday I might call upon you for support."

Van Loan smiled. "I'd be honored to back your plans, Jack, but take some advice. Finish college, meet a woman and have a family. It's the one thing that has escaped me so far."

Kennedy chuckled. "I read the rags, you know. You have no shortage of bathing beauties to pick from."

Van Loan conceded the point. It was true. Women threw themselves at him. He was handsome, rich and affable. Why then was he so lonely?

His thoughts turned to the lovely Muriel Havens who had pined for him since she was a teen.

"Jack, if someone had a problem in Boston. Say they needed to dig up some dirt on bad characters, where would they go?"

Kennedy didn't hesitate in his reply.

"Simple enough, start at the two hottest night clubs in town, Cocoanut Grove and Cotton Club. They used to be run by Charles Solomon, the rum runner affectionately known as King before someone rubbed him out a few years back. Local reporters tried to tie Pops into that racket, but my father is clean I'm telling you. He may have been photographed with some of those ruffians, but that's part of life. Power deals with power. Anyway, the clubs are legit now, but if something is stirring in town, Frankie the Rat will know."

"The rat?"

"Don't ask. I'll leave word with the doormen to take good care of you. You're in Boston, have some chowder and a few lobsters. Support our economy." He winked at the playboy. "Make sure you tell them Jack Kennedy sent you."

• • •

Richard Curtis Van Loan had called ahead and made reservations at the Hotel Manger. Built only a few years back at a cost of almost three million dollars, the luxurious building opened in 1930. Sporting over five hundred rooms, the state of the art tower served as the ground floor for radio station WMEX. It also boasted a direct connection to the Boston Garden which had opened only a few years back under the guidance of Tex Rickard for a whopping ten million dollars.

Jack Kennedy was absolutely correct. Boston was thriving, as were most of the east coast cities. The poverty and destruction still ravaged the Midwest of the country. The economy had shifted to construction and invention, a trend Joe Kennedy had shrewdly forecasted.

After a quick goodbye and a promise to keep in touch, Van Loan departed company with the suave Kennedy and headed into the swanky upscale Manger. Much to his surprise, the concierge greeted him by name.

"We've been expecting you Mr. Van Loan. Your presence honors us."

The man wore an immaculate black tuxedo, spiffy new loafers, and an expensive chain watch. He stood noble as he addressed Van Loan.

"I've taken the liberty of sending a bottle of our finest champagne up to your suite, sir, as well as complementary chilled shrimp. My name is Beckett and I'll be at your disposal during your stay. If you need anything, ring the front desk and ask for me."

Van Loan shook his hand and declined an onrushing bell hop. He could manage his meager suitcases without difficulty, and honestly didn't want to risk the chance of his briefcase spilling open.

"Anything going on at the Garden tonight?" he asked.

Beckett brightened up. He instantly produced a pair of tickets.

"All-star wrestling, sir. Crusher versus Dazzler. Enjoy it with our compliments."

Van Loan accepted the tickets as well as his room key and declined an escort to the elevator. The Kennedys had managed to wrangle up the penthouse for him.

The view from his room was spectacular. He could see most of the city, mainly the historic North End where Paul Revere's house resided as well as most of Charlestown. The massive windows offered a glimpse of the Boston Harbor causing Van Loan to shudder as he recalled his harrowing ride through the Sumner Tunnel.

It was still early. He didn't expect to take in the wrestling spectacle. He would drop off the tickets with some fortunate soul later on. Meanwhile, he wanted to take a nap before heading out to investigate the night club scene in hopes of discovering a clue to Muriel Havens' whereabouts. First, he wanted to check out the hotel's interior radio station.

A call down to the front desk brought Beckett dashing to the room within minutes. Van Loan assured him it was unnecessary for the personal visit, but the concierge insisted on it. A few minutes later, Beckett had arranged for a private tour of WMEX.

Van Loan couldn't believe the splendor of the private radio station. He actually owned two of them himself in Manhattan, but they were hidden away in cramped office buildings. This one here was flaunted like a showpiece with light bulbs everywhere. He actually felt himself blinking from the brightness.

The radio station manager, Morton Hill, was delighted to escort Van Loan around.

"This is a most fortunate day, Mr. Van Loan. A great deal of celebrities are in town for the Mass Handicap."

"Yes, it was delightful. Suffolk Downs was most impressive, as is your station I might add."

Hill nodded vigorously. "The best is yet to come. I'd like to introduce you to a very special guest we have visiting tonight to promote his national radio show. I'll keep it a secret, but I'll offer you a hint. He was born right here in Boston."

Van Loan smiled politely.

"I would love to meet a radio star."

Hill snorted. "Not just a radio star. The man's a movie star, a rather well known one. I ask that you please restrain any impulses you might have to assault him with a barrage of questions. I know what it's like when you first meet someone famous."

Van Loan continued smiling.

"I promise to be on my very best behavior."

Hill tugged at his jacket and straightened his tie before yanking on the studio door. With an extra bit of relish, he held the door closed for a few extra moments to examine Van Loan's eyes.

"I'll be good." Van Loan whispered.

Satisfied, Morton Hill swung the door the rest of the way.

A tall, lanky fellow, dressed casually in a crisp white buttoned down shirt and tan trousers turned around to greet them. His eyes widened when he saw Richard Curtis Van Loan.

"Dick Van Loan! You prankster, you sure do get around!" The man vigorously shook hands with Van Loan. "What brings you to Beantown?"

Before Van Loan could answer, Morton Hill interceded, a stunned expression blanketing his face.

"You two know each other?" the station manager blurted out.

"Richard and I go back sometime." The actor stated. "Boy the stories I could tell you about this guy!" He jabbed a hand at Van Loan's midsection. "I'm still not welcomed at Betty Grable's home because of you!"

Morton Hill realized his jaw was still open. He sheepishly closed it and frantically ran a hand through his few strands of hair.

"Beg your pardon Mr. Van Loan. Forgive me."

Van Loan gave him a queer look.

"Forgive you for what, my good man? You can't be expected to know everyone who struts through those doors. Besides, John here is the real draw."

The John that Van Loan was pointing at was better known to movie goers as Jack Haley known for his recent big hits with the aforementioned Betty Grable as well as America's sweetheart, Shirley Temple. A natural entertainer, Haley had just been awarded a radio show of his own.

"It's okay Morton," Haley instructed, "Why don't you give my friend the grand tour while I entertain your employees and sponsors, that is what I'm here for."

Morton obeyed. "Of course, Mr. Haley." He smiled oddly at Van Loan. "If you'll accompany me sir, I'll show you the rest of our fine establishment. We're not the biggest broadcaster out there but our antenna over on the hill in Charlestown allows us to reach a fair sized audience."

An expert on electronics, Van Loan was thrilled to take a peek at the latest broadcast equipment. He was getting carried away when he spotted a large wall clock. He had already spent an hour touring the grand studio. He was about to depart when Morton Hill paralyzed him with a statement.

"You're almost as obsessed with this stuff as that beautiful New York reporter was last week."

Van Loan bolted from his chair and sprung within inches of the man. Instinctively, Morton Hill shrunk back, bewildered by the eccentric millionaire.

"Did I anger you in some way, Mr. Van Loan? Please don't say anything to your friend Haley. He has a ton of clout with the owners and I have a family."

Van Loan grabbed the man by his collar. He could feel the sweat ooze onto his fingertips.

"What was the woman's name?"

Before the words even rolled off his lips, Van Loan knew what the response would be.

Muriel Havens had been here at radio station WMEX.

● ● ●

After a few more minutes of jostling around the frightened radio manager, Van Loan grew frustrated. He hadn't learned much. Muriel Havens and Steve Huston had indeed visited the interior of the radio station during their stay at the Manger. Being the daughter of a wealthy publisher, Muriel had been treated with the outmost respect during her tour of the station.

Morton Hill tried to nervously recall segments of their conversation. He kept insisting the girl asked standard questions that held little value or insight into what she was writing about. Van Loan persisted until he was actually forced to use the threat of violence to talk Hill into coercion. Finally, the nervous manager was able to offer up a tidbit of interest.

"Repeat that again!" Van Loan demanded, careful not to let his Phantom voice take over.

Hill bobbed his head frantically.

"Like I told you before. They were all standard radio questions I've answered a million times, except for that one odd inquiry she made."

Van Loan bared his teeth menacingly prompting the man to continue.

"She asked the weirdest question. She wanted to know if our signal could penetrate the depths of the harbor."

"Meaning what exactly?"

He gulped. "What she wanted to know is if the signal could be picked up underneath the water!"

Van Loan backed up hesitantly, trying to absorb the impact of the statement. What angle was Muriel working? Why was she curious about radio broadcasts and where had her investigation led to?

He thanked the grateful manager and departed back toward the hotel. On the way to the foyer, he spotted Jack Haley signing autographs and posing for photos. He stopped and whispered in his friend's ear.

"I will straighten things out with Betty when I see her for cocktails next weekend."

Haley flashed a wolfish grin.

"You do that, Dick."

With a wave of his hand, Van Loan departed from WMEX studios and made his way back into the ultra modern lobby of the Hotel Manger. Like a skilled magician, the concierge, Beckett, visualized before his eyes.

"I trust you enjoyed your tour of our fabulous studio?"

Van Loan considered and then responded. "It was insightful."

Beckett smiled an appreciative grin. "Where are you heading to next, sir? We can provide a vehicle at your service courtesy of Mr. Joseph Kennedy."

Van Loan glanced at his watch.

"I've been told I can't leave Boston without visiting the Cocoanut Grove and the Cotton Club."

Beckett nodded. "Both fine establishments, sir. Different forms of music but both feature an upscale clientele."

Van Loan grinned. "Well, that's my dilemma. I'm not looking for high and mighty."

"Beg your pardon sir?"

"I'm looking for a certain rodent named Frankie."

A curt smile surfaced on Beckett's contours.

"The rodent you refer to can be found at the Cotton Club tonight. Too far of a stroll I might add. I will summon a car."

"I will straighten things out with Betty..."

Van Loan waved him off.

"That won't be necessary, Beckett. I'm looking to be discreet."

The concierge cleared his throat and tapped his polished shoes together.

"We can accommodate all your needs here sir, but I understand a gentlemen who values the hunt."

Van Loan winked at him, happy that man assumed he was just a bored playboy trolling for easy women. It would be better that way, if trouble did occur and the Phantom needed to make an appearance. No one would suspect Richard Curtis Van Loan.

• • •

Turned out the Cotton Club was only a short journey to the inner city neighborhood known as Roxbury. Van Loan had hailed a cab after spending ten minutes outside the Boston Garden looking for some underprivileged children to hand off the wrestling tickets. He was informed that the West End kids were weary of handouts from strangers so he passed off the tickets to a couple of sailors who were in town and only more than happy to take them off his hands.

He had brought his briefcase containing his Phantom gear. Call it intuition or a hunch, but he felt it might come in handy later on.

He paid the taxi driver and stepped out in front of the celebrated night club. He chuckled, noticing the sweet shop next door.

The Cotton Club was a swank affair, catering to the musical taste of its mostly black clientele. Boston's Negro community were proud of their heritage and boasted a big enough audience to draw national acts. Count Basie, himself, had stopped by the night before after performing a set over in Maine at Orchid Beach.

The roomy interior was dark and filled with cigarette and cigar smoke. Van Loan didn't care for either. No matter, he wasn't here for the atmosphere. His intentions were to locate Frankie the Rat, and extract information regarding Muriel Havens' whereabouts.

The doorman stopped him with a gentle but firm hand on the shoulder.

"You'll have to go to the bar, sir. Tables are for couples only."

Van Loan nodded and started to proceed, only to be physically stopped again.

"The briefcase has to be checked sir, company policy."

Van Loan was prepared for this. Long ago, a magician had shown him how to separate his wares with a fake bottom. He flipped the latches and held the case out in front of him. The doorman inspected the wad of documents casually, before giving his approval.

"Welcome to the Cotton Club and enjoy your evening."

Richard sauntered over to the bar and ordered a club soda. He leaned back against the teakwood counter top and spoke to the bartender with his back turned to him.

"I need to see Frankie the Rat."

The bartender didn't look up from the counter.

"This is a proper joint mister. We don't have rats. It's against the board of health rules."

Van Loan still faced away from him. "Is that so?"

"Afraid it's true. Now why don't you enjoy the show."

Van Loan finally turned and locked eyes with the bartender. The man didn't flinch.

"Something else, bub?"

"As a matter of fact there is." Van Loan remarked. "I could have sworn my friend said this is where Frankie the Rat would be tonight."

The bartender was a red nosed Irishman from South Boston. He didn't scare easy.

"This friend of yours, did he leave his name?"

Van Loan smiled. "Sure did. Jack Kennedy, son of Joe Kennedy. Perhaps you heard of him?"

The color vanished from the bartender's face. He stopped cleaning the class he had in his hand and slammed it on the counter sternly.

"Wait here." He ordered.

Van Loan watched as the man marched over to a side table and addressed two men sitting at a table watching one of the jazz singers. The men glanced over at Van Loan before whispering something in the bartender's ear. The impatient bartender waved Van Loan over to the table.

"These gents would like to have a word with you." He told Van Loan before resuming his duties behind the bar.

Van Loan stood in front of the two men as passively as possible. His instinct was to throttle them for information, but he knew the club maintained a high profile, and he'd get nowhere fast with that tactic. He smiled at the gents.

"May I?" he asked, pointing at a chair.

The two well-dressed men appeared to be Italian, not much of a surprise. Kennedy had mentioned that the mob had moved in right after the assassination of King Solomon.

Neither man offered a reply, so Van Loan plopped his body into the chair.

"What's in the briefcase?" one of the men asked. He was overweight and puffing on a fat cigar which was causing his cheeks to bloat up.

"This briefcase?" Van Loan replied. "Just my paperwork."

The other man was slender and had his hair slicked back. His hands were well manicured and his clothes were a bit pompous. He was the complete opposite of his partner.

"Heard you were asking about Frankie?"

Van Loan nodded.

"What do you need to see him about?"

"That's private."

The skinny man wrangled his fingers together and crossed his legs in frustration.

"Is he here?" Van Loan asked.

The dandy stared at his heavyset partner. Neither spoke, but that was okay with Van Loan. Their silence spoke volumes.

Finally the other man spoke up in a gruff voice.

"Frankie ain't seeing visitors tonight. Leave your name and a number we can reach you at and maybe tomorrow someone might contact you."

Van Loan grinned. "I don't like the word maybe. It's usually followed by not, as in maybe not."

The skinny man pursed his lips and glared at Van Loan.

"What are you a wise guy? Do you know who runs this place?"

Van Loan saw an opportunity and seized it.

"Obviously a relative of yours, because no one else could take you seriously with that oil slick on top of your head."

The slender man cringed and waved a fist at Van Loan.

"Don't do that." Van Loan cautioned. "It's embarrassing to look at you."

This incensed the man to his boiling point. He turned to his chubby partner in desperation. The blob was already in action. He raised his hand signaling for the bouncers. Two burly black men dressed in neat suits came over. They said nothing but grabbed Van Loan under the armpits. He didn't resist.

"These gentlemen will escort you to the street. You will not return here, ever. Understand?" the bloated man barked.

Van Loan nodded, remaining calm. He reached out for his briefcase, but a small hand slapped it away. It was the prissy man.

"No, that stays here. Maybe you'll get it back someday, but not tonight."

Van Loan sighed. He hadn't planned on this type of reception. Jack Kennedy must have overestimated his clout.

"I can't leave here without my case," he said in a soft tone.

The skinny man smiled an evil grin. He snapped his fingers at the guards, a signal that the conversation had been terminated. Van Loan felt his feet leave the ground. The two dark skinned bouncers carried him with little effort.

"Ha ha!" the little man gloated to his chubby friend. "This chump will never make that mistake again."

Van Loan ignored him. He could not let his forensic kit fall into an outsider's hand. It contained his Phantom outfit and could reveal his true identity. He had to act, and fast.

He stomped his left foot down on the foot of the man on his left, who instantly released his grip. In that split second, Van Loan dropped to a crouch and swung his leg around the wounded man, sweeping him off his feet. A quick thrust to the man's throat disabled him.

The other bouncer reacted predictably, charging like a bull at Van Loan. The athletic playboy countered the move by springing out of his crouch and delivering a quick blow to the giant's solar plexus. The man stood frozen, a look of confusion on his face, before toppling over backwards, the air having been forced from his lungs.

Van Loan stalked over to the table. The whimsical man loosened his grip on the briefcase. His jaw was hanging open. Van Loan thought about smashing a fist against it, but decided against it. Instead, he simply snatched his briefcase and rushed through the throng that had gathered during the commotion.

He was like a college fullback, weaving through traffic, fighting for space. Finally, he emerged into the moonlight and stopped to see if he was being followed. To his relief, no one was coming from the night club. He was about to depart in search of a taxi, when a bright spotlight stung his eyes.

It was coming from a parked car at the curb. Van Loan tensed, wondering if he was about to be gunned down. He heard the car door open, and a middle aged man, dressed casually, but neatly emerged from the vehicle. He held both arms up to show Van Loan he was unarmed.

"Heard you been looking for me?" the man called out. "I'm Frankie the Rat."

• • •

Frankie the Rat was one Francis Albert Pagliuca, part time gangster, full time snitch. When the Italian mob had usurped power from the Irish gangs a few years back, Pagliuca had got shorted in his reward for his part in the overthrow. As a result, he had turned bitter and become an informant for the Irish interests. Like most political heavyweights, the Kennedy family kept ears on the ground, and thus Frankie the Rat had become a valuable source of information for the influential family. His devotion to Joseph Kennedy was unbreakable.

"Jackie called and vouched for you. His word is good enough for me," Pagliuca explained. "Get in my car. We can talk while I give you a ride home."

Van Loan hesitated, his eyes still on the doorway to the Cotton Club. At that moment, the weasel faced thug and his overweight partner bolted from the entrance with their two dark skinned bodyguards in tow. Van Loan braced himself for action.

The quartet came to a halt when they saw Frankie Pagliuca emerge from the shadows. Frankie said nothing. He simply pointed at one of the bouncers and curled a finger for the man to approach. The burly bodyguard stiffened up and strolled over to hold a private conversation with Frankie. Van Loan strained his ears but couldn't eavesdrop on the conversation.

A moment later, Frankie dismissed the big lout and waved over the slender, girlish man. The mobster hesitated until his fat friend shoved him forward. Apparently, Frankie the Rat was not someone to be denied. The skinny man tiptoed his way over to Frankie, only to be promptly greeted by a vicious backhand across the face.

Van Loan groaned. He knew this display was all for his benefit. He wanted to intervene but knew better. Discipline was a code of the streets. The man had made a mistake and was being punished.

"Sorry, Frankie!"

Frankie slapped him with the other hand, hard enough to leave a welt.

"Not me you simpleton. This is Richard Curtis Van Loan from New York. He is to be treated with the outmost respect while he visits our fine establishments. Mr. Van Loan is a guest of our fine city, and if anything should happen to him while he is visiting, there will be consequences." The later part of this statement was directed to all four men.

The slick haired Italian bobbed his head up and down in acknowledgement and then turned heel and raced back into the safety of the Cotton Club. His overweight accomplice simply tipped his hat at Van Loan before following his friend. The two black bouncers remained outside until Van Loan entered the waiting vehicle.

Frankie the Rat slid into the backseat with him. An older, rough looking gent was behind the steering wheel. He waited for instructions.

"I'm staying at the Manger," Van Loan offered.

The old thug glanced in the rear view mirror at Frankie the Rat who nodded his consent. The old timer released the clutch and headed back to the West End.

Van Loan cleared his throat. "Thanks for the rescue."

Frankie the Rat lit the stub of a cigar and inhaled a large puff before offering Van Loan a fresh one. Van Loan waved it off as they barreled down Tremont Street.

"Jackie said you might need some information," Frankie prompted.

"I'm looking for a reporter, Muriel Havens. She works for the *Clarion* out of New York. She's also the publisher's daughter and a close friend of mine."

Frankie nodded. "So what's the deal with this close friend?"

"She arrived in Boston with a colleague, Steve Huston, to investigate a tip a few days back. No one has heard from either of them since."

"Maybe they got cozy together. Boston is a romantic city."

Van Loan stifled his anger. "They're both professionals," he answered, ignoring the accusation. "It's standard procedure to check-in."

"What have you picked up so far?"

"Not much," Van Loan admitted. "Just one clue. They were at radio station WMEX investigating whether or not the broadcast signal could be heard from underneath the water."

Frankie squinted. "Music for the fish?"

"Not sure what it means, but my hunch is underwater vessels."

"Submarines?"

Van Loan didn't reply. Frankie the Rat inhaled a deeper lungful of the pungent cigar and sat back in the coupe. He rubbed a hand across his stubby chin.

"Every once in a while I come across news that don't make no sense at first but then something clicks."

Van Loan's interest was peaked. "What do you mean?"

"Boston's a big town but still under the control of very few factions. As such, word gets around when someone new tries to muscle into the picture. Obviously, you got your politicians and law enforcements, as well as the Irish and Italians, but lately I hear a lot of chatter."

"About what?"

Frankie rolled down the window and unceremoniously tossed out the cigar stub.

"Word has it the Chinese have been asking around town about the harbor a lot. Now mind you, they've always had their yellow hands involved in the smuggling business, so it's not odd when they ask about shipping schedules, and general wharf questions, but lately their inquiries have been bizarre."

"Meaning what exactly?"

"That's just it," said Frankie the Rat." Word has it they been real interested in radio signals and all that."

Van Loan saw the Boston Garden come into view. The elderly driver slowed down the vehicle. Patrons were emerging from the venue, excited from a night of wrestling.

"Any idea who I should talk to in Chinatown?"

Frankie laughed so hard, snot dripped from his nose.

"White men have no place in Boston's Chinatown. This isn't New York or San Francisco. These people still hold a grudge because of the immigration halt. The mayor allows them to their space because they pay their taxes and all, but it's almost like a private city over there so you can forget about that."

"Thanks anyhow." Van Loan said, not deterred. He had no intention of infiltrating Chinatown as a white man. "You can drop me off here."

Again the old timer glanced in the rear view mirror. Frankie the Rat nodded and the gentlemen pulled over to the curb. He didn't bother shutting off the engine. Van Loan began to open the door, when an arm gripped his wrist. Frankie had stopped him.

"Something to add?" he asked.

Frankie smiled. 'You strike me as the type who doesn't take no for an answer."

Van Loan remained motionless, waiting for the informant to continue.

"Anyway," Frankie started, "If someone was to ask questions around Chinatown, the man to talk to is Li Cheung, runs a chicken outlet." He released his grip on the wrist.

Van Loan said nothing as he departed from the vehicle. He hardly had a foot on the pavement before the coupe peeled away. He entered the swanky hotel lobby. Much to his chagrin, Beckett was still on duty at the front desk. The concierge flashed great energy when he bolted from behind the corner.

"Hope you enjoyed your evening, Mr. Van Loan?"

Richard Van Loan was exhausted, but managed a friendly smile. "Boston sure is a beehive of activity." He remarked.

Beckett beamed as if the compliment was directed at him.

"No finer city in America," he proclaimed.

Van Loan nodded and began to walk to the elevator. He turned around, only to discover Beckett less than two feet away from him.

"Yes, sir?"

"I need to get to a department store tomorrow to pick up some goods."

"I'll have a driver ready, sir."

Van Loan shook his head. "No, I'll walk. Anything close by?"

"Absolutely. One of the finest in the country right down the way on Washington Street. You can't miss it, Raymond's Department store."

Van Loan nodded and entered the elevator. "Good night, Mr. Beckett."

The door swished close as the car ascended to the penthouse where Richard Curtis Van Loan would replenish his energy with a good night's sleep.

• • •

The next morning, Van Loan woke refreshed from a well-earned sleep and after enjoying the comfort of a swim in the hotel's pool, dined on a lavish breakfast consisting of heaping portions of eggs, ham, and toast. His body fueled up for a trek, he exited the elevator on his way out of the building. Much to his surprise, Beckett wasn't on duty.

"So you are human after all" he mumbled exiting the Manger for his short stroll up to Washington Street.

The New England weather was known for being finicky. Turned out the heat-wave was short lived. The air was milder today with a pleasant breeze blowing in from the waterfront. Van Loan was glad he had walked.

Making his way past City Hall on School Street, his ears perked up as he began to hear the strains of a banjo playing.

"Hillbilly music in Boston?" he muttered.

His wonderment continued as he turned onto the corner of busy Washington Street just in time to witness a spectacle: a caravan of people, garbed as villagers, were marching down the pathway following a slow moving hayrick being pulled by an oxen. The villagers were shouting and teasing the onlookers by tossing pails of confetti at them.

Van Loan noticed an elderly gent sitting on a stool he had apparently brought with him to view the parade.

"What gives?" Van Loan asked.

Without taking his eyes off the astounding group, the old timer answered politely. "They're headed for Toonerville! Same as every year."

Van Loan didn't bother to question the event. He had specific plans for the morning.

"Can you tell me where Raymond's is located?"

The elderly man guffawed and turned his wrinkled face around for a better look.

"You ain't from around these parts?" he didn't wait for an answer. "Just follow the villagers. That's where the parade always ends."

"At Raymond's?"

"Toonerville." When the man saw the look of confusion on Van Loan's face, he clarified. "Toonerville is inside of Raymond's."

Van Loan tried to absorb the information.

"Boston is a hotbed of activity! Why are these folks all decked out like farmhands?"

The old man rose off his stool.

"Don't you know what day it is, son?" Again, he didn't wait for a reply. "It's Unkle Eph day!"

The name was pronounced like EEF.

Van Loan nodded as if he understood. "Do they sell art supplies?"

The old man nodded. "If you can't find something at Raymond's, then it can't be found in Boston! Now if you don't mind, I'd like to watch what's left of the parade."

Van Loan thanked the man and headed off behind the rear of the marching villagers. As the parade wound down and they approached Raymond's he could see a huge banner hanging from the window of the gigantic department store. It read, "Home of Unkle Eph."

To the side he could see another sign stating Unkle Eph's Food Shop. In front of it stood a throng of people, hundreds deep. They were all craning their necks to get a better view of a gentlemen addressing them at a podium.

"Please be patient." The man was yelling into a bullhorn. "Unkle Eph wants to visit with all of you but we can only accommodate so many folk at once inside our humble store."

Van Loan marveled at this understatement. The department store was huge, clearly an anchor for the shopping district.

The well-dressed man continued to address the crowd, reminding them to stop at all sections of the store today for surprises and performances from the villagers.

Van Loan noticed a group of wealthy men standing inside the roped off area, laughing and shaking hands. Among them was young Jack Kennedy, pressing the flesh and still blinding people with his affable smile. He spotted Van Loan and buffaloed his way through the group.

"Dick, didn't know you were here today. Making an investment?"

Van Loan smiled as he shook the enthusiastic youngster's hand. Kennedy motioned for one of the security personnel to allow his friend to enter.

"I'm actually here to make a purchase," Van Loan stated. "I was told this is the place to find something."

Kennedy grinned. "Couldn't be more true, but you can't come to Unkle Eph day without meeting the main attraction himself."

"You mean there really is an Unkle Eph?"

Kennedy excused himself from his followers and led Van Loan into the main floor of the massive department store. Customers had flooded the area to catch a glimpse of the famous character. Van Loan could see why.

Sitting high above the stage, on an elevated platform, stood a brightly colored man with a snowy beard, white whiskers, an oversized watch chain and a truly unique vest covered with ribbons.

The crowd, many of them children, were beaming at the man in adoration as a few of the parade marchers circled around banging on drums and other instruments.

A security guard spotted Jack Kennedy and ushered the men forward to what amounted to a throne.

Unkle Eph climbed down from his chair to greet Kennedy. Van Loan could tell the man had the outmost respect for the younger Kennedy.

"This is Richard Curtis Van Loan." Kennedy announced without any fanfare.

Unkle Eph shook hands encouragingly.

"I read all the trades Van Loan. Your business intellect is always mentioned. I hope you not here to open a department store in Boston?" He was only half joking.

Van Loan assured him his intentions lay elsewhere.

The two men exchanged some quiet banter before Kennedy prompted them to separate so the customers could meet their idol. Van Loan exchanged business cards and moved away from the gathering.

Kennedy arranged a special escort for the millionaire to browse the art department privately. Before Van Loan could protest, a fleet of salesmen shuffled him away. He barely had time to thank his young benefactor.

Inside the expansive arts department, Van Loan filled up a basket with an assortment of sponges, dyes, liquids, glue and anything else he might need for his project. He started to head for the register when a sales clerk waved him off.

"Mr. Kennedy insists on covering your tab sir. Enjoy your day at Raymond's."

Van Loan thanked the clerk and headed past the throng back to the main entrance. On the way he stopped in the children's section and fished out a pile of dollar bills. He quietly slipped around the room, handing each youngster he could find one of the greenbacks.

After exhausting a thick wad of cash, he departed from Raymond's into the mild air and began the leisurely stroll back to the lavish Hotel Manger.

• • •

Upon entering the luxurious hotel lobby, Van Loan was greeted by Beckett, the concierge.

"Good day, Mr. Van Loan."

"Beckett."

The sharp eyed man spotted Van Loan's shopping bag.

"I see you found Raymond's. I trust they had what you sought?"

Van Loan nodded. "They did. And you could have given me a heads up about Unkle Eph day."

Beckett snorted in exaggeration. "And ruin your surprise?"

The handsome playboy flashed a wry grin. He liked this man. He appreciated the pride the fellow took in his position.

"I have a special request," he stated.

Beckett nodded curtly. "I'm at your assistance."

"I need a pair of scissors, very sharp ones that can cut through fabric."

Beckett tightened his tie. "I'll deliver them personally sir."

A few moments later, Van Loan was inside the comfort of the penthouse suite. He picked up the phone and had the operator connect him with the Clarion Building in New York. A minute later, Frank Havens was on the line, huffing deeply. He must have sprinted for the phone.

"Any word on my baby?" he demanded.

Van Loan didn't mince words. "Nothing yet, sir." He answered in the deep monotone of the Phantom.

Frank Havens stuttered his reply. "Do you think? I mean, do…"

The Phantom cut him off. "I only can go by facts. She was here investigating a radio station. I'm following a lead. I will be in touch."

"Thank you, Phantom." Frank Havens answered but the line was already dead.

Seconds later, a firm wrap knocked on the door. Van Loan peered through the eyehole before opening the door for Beckett. Like a trooper, the concierge had come through. He handed over a huge pair of shears without questions. Van Loan reached for his wallet, but Beckett slowly shook his head.

"Managers are requested not to accept tips, sir, but feel free to reward our hardworking bellhops and room maids."

Van Loan thanked him and settled down on the expensive velvet chair. He recalled the name Frankie the Rat had supplied him with. Time to pay a visit to Li Cheung.

• • •

No one paid any attention to the fleet footed Chinaman exiting the laundry room of the Hotel Manger's basement. Had the patrons or employees examined him more carefully, they would have noticed his apparel looked awfully familiar.

The Phantom had used the shears to cut up the expensive silk drapes into a makeshift robe. He had then emptied the contents of his Raymond's shopping back onto the king size bed and within minutes had completed a startling transformation.

Using the sponges, a light yellow dye and a washcloth, Phantom had altered his skin color to resemble the patina of an Asian. He had shaved off most of his eyebrows and using a fine marker, drew new narrow ones. To these he attached invisible tape which slanted his eyes upward, giving him different facial features. He also stuffed cotton balls under his upper lip to make his jawline protrude. The final touch was achieved by ripping the hair from a child's doll and weaving it into two different halves of a mustache which he applied to his face using spirit glue.

Overall the effect was chilling. No one would have recognized Phantom as a Caucasian and most certainly not as millionaire playboy Richard Curtis Van Loan.

Forcing himself to walk without his usual gaping strides, the Phantom shuffled out of the building and headed for the subway station. He didn't dare use a cab, nor did he want to risk the heat disrupting his disguise. Moments later, he boarded Boston's public transportation on his way to Chinatown.

• • •

...the fleet footed Chinaman exiting the laundry room...

Van Loan squished himself into a crowded subway car for the brief ride to Chinatown. The car was jammed with passengers and the air was a bit stifling, but nothing compared to what he had endured traveling the frightening Sumner Tunnel. Before he knew it, he had emerged onto Washington Street, surprisingly not far from where he had shopped at Raymond's Department Store.

Unlike New York and San Francisco's commercially geared Chinatowns, the residents of Boston had not broken down the racial barriers yet. The Asian community had been stunted earlier in the century when Americans had prevented the influx of more Chinese onto the shores. As a result, the Chinese people had not blended in as well as the other cultures that had sought refuge in the United States. The Chinese stuck to themselves, adamant to keep the old customs and languages. Only recently, had the success of San Francisco's huge tourist income inspired Asians to start luring the white man's money.

Fortunately, Van Loan was a well-traveled businessman. He had acquired a decent working knowledge of Mandarin, certainly enough to communicate in a boardroom. He would have to keep his words at a minimum and his concentration at a premium.

Within minutes, luck favored the Phantom. He spotted a small storefront selling chickens in the window. Much to his relief the sign out front matched the name Frankie the Rat had given him. The Phantom smoothed out his fake mustache and made sure the tape on his eyes remained glued before swinging open the door to the open market.

He was assaulted by a bevy of smells hitting his senses. The livestock was uncaged. Chickens hopped wildly among the customers, many of them pecking at prospective buyers. Phantom nearly wretched from the odor of feces and mildew. There was no way local health inspectors had visited this shop in the recent past.

Much to his relief, he was ignored, free to roam around, as the other customers nudged each other out of the way, anxious to make their purchase and leave the fetid area.

Phantom craned his neck to get a look past the main room beyond a partially closed curtain. He made out several butchers chopping chickens to death while elderly Chinese women scooped up the headless corpse and inserted it in a bag for purchase. The heads remained on the dusty floor, hopefully to be removed later.

He eyed a doorway leading to basement steps. He tried to inch closer for a better view but was met by a resisting hand. One of the bloody butchers shouted at him in mandarin that the area was confined to employees only.

"Thank god for that!" Phantom thought.

He turned and pretended to sort through a clucking batch of chickens when he saw two sharp dressed Asians enter the shop. They both wore sunglasses and neither man said anything as they shuffled into the back-room. Both customers and employees moved aside hurriedly as the men advanced. Phantom watched curiously as the two men opened the base-ment door and descended.

He waited five minutes but neither man emerged.

Phantom was intrigued. Why were two well-dressed men entering a slaughterhouse only to visit the basement? It was a question not likely to be answered during the broad daylight. He decided to return later during the cover of darkness when the Phantom Detective operated best!

• • •

The Phantom Detective returned to Chinatown during the undercover of darkness. The tiny section of Boston was quiet, the subdued denizens of Chinatown not adhering to the glitzy nightlife of their counterparts in New York. Phantom was able to move at will among the shadows.

His photographic memory recalled the layout of the poultry market and from his vantage point a frontal entrance would be too risky. Instead, the Phantom clawed his way past the rodent filled dumpsters in the back alleyway until he located the back entrance. One forceful kick knocked in the rectangular window at the base of the pavement.

Phantom tucked his shoulders in close and leaned into the open space. Past practice had taught him wisely not to jump into action. Many propri-etors countered break-ins by setting up traps under the windows, ranging from elaborate cages to mundane shards of broken glass. Phantom had a small flashlight between his teeth, which would allow him to spy any such devices.

The flashlight probably saved his life. He felt a rush of hot breath on his face before a snarling set of jaws snapped at his chin. Only the Phantom's lightning face reflexes saved him from disfigurement. As it was the giant creature had ripped the flashlight in half!

The brief light enabled the Phantom to capture a fleeting image of the animal. It was a massive Rottweiler. It thrust its head up in vain, trying savagely to tear at Phantom's flesh. The detective pulled back, fortunate that the animal was too big to follow.

The Phantom's gray fedora had fallen into the darkness of the basement, causing the disturbed animal to gnaw on it in anticipation of a greater conquest.

Instinctively, the Phantom withdrew a capsule from the lining of his overcoat and tossed it through the window. The minute capsule struck the basement floor and released a fast spreading gas. The capsule contained an anesthesia which would evaporate in less than a minute. Phantom silently ticked off the seconds and then satisfied the brute was unconscious, contorted his frame to slip through the small opening.

He landed on his feet in the darkness, wishing his flashlight had not been ravaged by the attacking animal. The pale moonlight threw a tiny sliver of light on the area, but not enough for Phantom to make his way safely through the basement.

Phantom again reached into his coat. This time he withdrew a small twisted sack from the lining. He raised it above his head and brought it down forcefully on the basement floor.

Immediately a powdered flash lit up the room if only for a brief instance. This was time enough for the Phantom's keen senses to memorize the layout. He quickly made his way to a light switch on the wall and flipped it on.

Brilliant light blanketed the room. Phantom quickly removed his coat and draped it across the window opening to avoid any spying neighbors. He then turned and surveyed the room. His eyes settled on the gigantic Rottweiler.

"Sorry boy," he patted the sleeping dog's head.

Phantom slowly spun and absorbed the layout of the room. The walls were covered with nautical maps. There were dozens of them encompassing each major seaport along the east coast. Many of the maps had huge red circles drawn on them. Phantom scanned each map carefully until he located one detailing the Boston harbor.

The map was marked up with a giant red circle around the Charlestown section of Boston, which was only minutes away from the Hotel Manger.

Phantom's photographic memory recalled a brochure he had studied in the hotel's lobby. That particular section of the city was home to the coast guard, naval bases and the final destination of the U.S.S. Constitution!

A chill went down Phantom's spine. He raced to the other maps and scanned them thoroughly. All of the circled areas were naval yards! Something was amiss! Muriel Havens must have stumbled upon some nefarious espionage!

• • •

The Boston Naval Yard in Charlestown was base of operations for the construction of the United State's military vessels. The engineers of the base had launched the USS Ralph Talbot the year before and were currently building the USS Mayrant. The yard itself was heavily fortified and maintained a four story barrack filled with deadly trained US marines.

Phantom ventured Muriel had uncovered something of value regarding the security of our country. His heart raced faster as he headed toward the Naval Yard. This would have to be a mission for the Phantom Detective. Even though the country was at peace, no civilians were allowed on the base, not even someone with the stature of Richard Curtis Van Loan.

The Phantom surveyed the area from above the rooftops. His grappling hook held tight as he rallied from building to building searching for clues or hints. It was not until he reached the end of the district that he took time to rest.

The sun would be up soon and the Phantom would lose the element of surprise. Frantically, he searched his mind for answers. He had checked the Marine barracks as well as the construction area around dry-dock. Both were heavily fortified with officers and Phantom dismissed the chances of wrong doing taking place there.

In the background he could see Old Ironsides, herself, the USS Constitution. A flag went up in Phantom's head. He had an uncanny sixth sense, honed from years of experience. The vessel itself served as an inspiration for Americans, a symbol of their triumph for independence. It would serve as a perfect target for those seeking to terrorize Americans.

Phantom swooped down from his hiding spot, careful to avoid the spotlights. A pair of sentry guards stood outside the magnificent warship, patrolling its exterior. Even though the ship hadn't seen active duty in ages, it had never been decommissioned and thus was afforded full military honors. Phantom knew those guards were instructed to shoot to kill.

He stared at the surroundings. The ship was anchored against the wharf, not buildings within range for an aerial descent and with the guards marching at the entrance; he would need an alternative pathway. He concentrated, as the silence of the night was only shattered by the occasional sound of waves rolling against the side of the Constitution.

"That's it!" Phantom thought. 'I'll make a watery entrance."

Phantom removed his topcoat and rolled it up. His fedora had been destroyed by the Rottweiler earlier. He removed his shoes and socks but left his domino mask on. Quietly, he moved amongst the shadows until he was at the wharf's edge. He counted slowly as he studied the guard's rotation of marching. They were synchronized within seconds of each other, covering all sides of the venue. Phantom noticed a three second lapse before they reached his hiding spot.

Timing it to the precise moment, Phantom plunged into the water a split second before the sentry turned the corner. The guard heard the slight splash and moved closer for inspection. He saw nothing on the surface of the water and dismissed it as an incoming wave. Satisfied, the enlisted man continued his duties.

Meanwhile, Phantom swam under the warm water until he reached the unexposed side of the Constitution. He located a hanging rope and with a mighty effort pulled himself up as quickly as possible. Flipping over the railing, he hit the deck and lay as still as possible.

Satisfied that his motions had gone undetected, Phantom surveyed the top deck. Nothing seemed amiss. He had gathered that from his observations above the building rooftops. If something was taking place aboard the vessel, it was happening on the lower deck.

Phantom shimmied across the wooden plank boards, careful to stay submerged in the darkness. He crawled on his belly until he arrived at the doorway to the lower deck. Phantom grabbed ahold of the railing and acrobatically flipped himself down the narrow stairway.

The Constitution had been constructed centuries earlier, and as thus, had not taken into consideration the height of someone like the Phantom. In the darkness, he struck his head on the low ceiling. The thud was hardly discernible, but it was enough to arouse some movement in the darkened cabin.

Phantom could barely hear the audible murmur coming from the corner.

"Should have carried a second flashlight!" he whispered. Even his pouch of magician flashes would be useless. They had gotten soaked during the swim.

Careful not to hit his head again, Phantom crawled on all fours toward the mumbling sounds. At one point he felt something furry scramble against his legs.

"Water rats!" he gasped.

Undaunted, Phantom continued to edge closer to the struggling sounds. At last his hands made contact with something. He felt the smooth feel of nylon against his fingertips. He could feel the warmth of human flesh exuding from beneath it.

Phantom shivered at the touch. Female!

"Muriel?" he uttered in a desperate tone.

The bound person beside him couldn't speak, but struggled against her restraints. Phantom reached out in the pitch darkness and located her face. Soft skin brushed against his fingertips before he tore the gag from her mouth.

Muriel inhaled several deep breaths, almost choking during the effort.

"Thank you! Thank you!" she shouted.

She couldn't see her rescuer. Phantom was happy about that. Without his hat and topcoat only the domino mask hid his identity, and he severely doubted that would be enough to fool an investigative reporter like Muriel.

He wanted so badly to hug her, to take her in his arms and kiss her, but he couldn't. The Phantom's anonymity was too valuable to risk.

"Pipe down! I don't want the sentries to know I'm present." Phantom ordered in his deep baritone.

Muriel composed herself. "My arms and legs are bound." A thought came to her. "Oh my god! Where is Steve?"

Phantom remembered that Steve Huston had accompanied her on her trip.

"I'll find him, but first let me free you."

Phantom tore at her restraints, his powerful hands shredding the taut ropes with ease.

"You are Muriel Havens?" he asked.

"Yes! And that voice! You are the Phantom Detective!"

"Miss Havens, what is going on?"

Muriel rubbed at her chaffed wrists in the darkness. She was in agony from the lack of circulation.

"I received a report that spies were in Boston gathering naval secrets and selling them to European powers!"

Phantom considered this.

"How were they smuggling the secrets out of the country?"

Muriel coughed her lips dry from lack of water.

"Radio broadcasts in code, designed to penetrate the water and reach hidden submarines!" she barked.

Phantom gritted his teeth. "Let me take a wild guess. The signals were emanating from radio station WMEX?"

"That's right! Steve and I were able to get a tour of the station and it didn't take long before we figured out something was wrong. Then I just remember getting sleepy and waking up in this dark hold with all sorts of dreadful things crawling across my body!"

Instinctively, she hugged Phantom. Although, the arid air had dried her skin, he could still inhale faint traces of her perfume. It made the Phantom long for her even more.

"Do you remember what happened? Did they use knockout gas?"

Muriel was silent in the darkness.

"Miss Havens, please try to recall. This is a matter of national security."

Muriel responded.

"No, the manager, Mr. Hill, was an extremely likable fellow. He had sandwiches and lemonade brought in for us, and..."

Phantom cut her off. "Probably laced with sedatives."

Muriel gasped. "Come to think of it, Mister Hill was awfully talkative. Steve and I just wanted to ask a few questions about the local bases when he insisted we join him for lunch. I never thought twice about it."

Phantom arose carefully not to strike his head again.

"I'm going to alert the guards to your whereabouts. Remain here and stay calm. These young men are trained snipers. Don't make any sudden moves at all and keep calm."

Muriel was bewildered.

"Where are you going?"

Phantom didn't answer. He had already departed. Muriel heard the sound of splashing as if someone had dove into the water.

• • •

Morton Hill neatly stacked the bills he was counting and then carefully wrapped rubber bands around each huge wad. He was packing up his money. Word had reached him that sources were onto his scheme to broadcast signals to German U-boats off the coast of Boston.

Hill had claimed a tidy sum from his profit and would have made more if it wasn't for that nosey dame, Muriel Havens, and her enchanting gams. Hill was a sucker for a beautiful woman, and the delightful New Yorker had entranced him with her pleasant looks and wholesome image. He hadn't planned on answering all her questions, but his loose tongue had gotten the best of him. When he realized he had been too talkative, he had been forced to drug her and her strong armed companion Huston.

No one would suspect the captives to be stored on the bottom hull of the USS Constitution. At least that was what he thought, but he learned from a source that Frankie the Rat was blabbing and that was enough for Hill.

The last stack of bills accounted for; he snapped the lid of his briefcase closed. Time to flee. He had a boat waiting for him down by the wharf. His European friends had assured him safe passage out of the country.

Hill gave his room one last glance before opening the door on his way to exile. He didn't get far.

A masked man stood in his doorway, dripping water from his drenched clothing.

"What the?" Morton Hill managed before a fist hammered into his face.

The bloated radio station manager dropped instantly to the floor, his eyes rolled back into his head.

Phantom calmly entered the room and tore up the bedsheet. He bound and gagged the traitorous manager to a chair and smugly took the briefcase.

Hill gave him a desperate glare. Phantom grinned and snapped off the ceiling fan. Let the puke swelter a little bit longer.

• • •

Richard Curtis Van Loan entered the lobby of the Hotel Manger minutes later just as sunrise took place. He was soaking wet and barefoot. He had discarded the domino mask. All he carried was a briefcase.

The concierge, Beckett, raced from behind the counter.

"Mr. Van Loan, is everything okay?" he asked in a concerned voice.

Van Loan nonchalantly wrung out the bottom of his shirt on the immaculate floor.

"Just fine, my good man. Just getting back from a refreshing swim in the harbor. You really must try it. Never know what you might find."

He took the briefcase and snapped it open for the amazed concierge.

"I believe the police will want to claim this cash. It was part of a payout from European powers to an American traitor you know very well, WMEX manager, Morton Hill."

Beckett stood mouth agape. He stared at the puddle on the floor.

"Should I have a clerk run out to get you some new shoes sir?"

Van Loan smiled. "That would be nice. Put it on my account. I'd also like you to have a couple of bottles of your finest champagne sent up to my room. I will be having company later."

"The individual you were seeking?" Beckett inquired against his training.

"Safe and sound." Van Loan replied. He waddled over to the elevator. "Oh, and Beckett?"

"Yes, Mr. Van Loan?"

"Those wonderful drapes that were in my room?"

"Yes, sir?"

Van Loan grinned as he pressed the elevator button.

"I disposed of them."

Beckett cast him a raised eyebrow.

"Yes," Van Loan elaborated, "Too Oriental for my taste. Have a decorator replace them and add it to my bill."

Beckett nodded, too much of a professional to make further inquiries. "Anything else sir?"

Van Loan pondered. "What's taking place at the Garden tonight?"

THE END

Harbor Lights

This story was more about the evolution of the city of Boston than The *Phantom Detective.* I was always in awe of the way Boston rose from the shadows of the depression to become a leader in economic development during the latter part of the 1930s. It all began as a domino effect with the building of the Sumner Tunnel, spurring the birth of Suffolk Downs racetrack, which was able to lure Seabiscuit for a race that would result in the largest purse and attendance in the stadium. During the same period, the Boston Garden and its connecting hotel, the Manger, with its in-house radio station, brought in throngs of acts which created revenue and jobs for the area. Storefronts, such as Raymonds, thrived on this influx of spending, which in a few short decades would propel a bright young adventurer into the White House.

I was able to come up with a plausible reason for the Phantom Detective to travel to this great city, and it gave me the opportunity to gift him with an expensive Bugatti plane. I enjoy both classic and modern versions of Phantom Detective and was finally able to craft a story around this fine character.

• • •

ROBERT RICCI - was born and raised in Boston, Massachusetts. A steady diet of Doc Savage novels and classic comic strip reprints shaped his love for the genre. A graduate of Curry College, he works in the computer industry. He is the author of Blood on the Cobblestones, the first in a modern pulp series featuring his creation, Jenna Coyne.

The Devil's Minions
by Gary Lovisi

Although none of them knew his identity, and most had never seen him, every member of the New York Police Department had heard of The Phantom; sometimes dubbed The Phantom Detective by the press. Most cops were even grateful to him for more than one piece of work that solved unsolvable crimes. Yet there were some who were not so thankful.

The scene is dark, foreboding, a pitch black alley in an exclusive but quiet part of the great city. Ernie Bilks, career criminal, proud second-story man, has just made the haul of a lifetime in precious jewelry after rifling the safe of the famed Ascot Hotel. Now he is leaving the scene of the crime with his ill-gotten gains climbing down the fire escape to the street below to make his getaway.

The night black figure in the slouch hat with a black silk mask across his eyes to hide his identity, is watching the scene above him with intense interest. It is the Phantom Detective, aka rich dilettante playboy Richard Curtis Van Loan, who is standing by ready to take down another of his cities' criminals and place him into custody. Then his attention is suddenly drawn by the image of a large man just entering the alley.

"A policeman?" Van Loan whispers to himself thoughtfully as he notes the uniformed man but continues to watch the thief descend the hotel fire escape onto the ground below. Then he looks more closely at the cop, who continues to walk calmly forward step-by-step, deeper into the alley. It is apparent that the cop will soon discover the thief and apprehend him, in what for a policeman on a beat would be a pretty good night's work.

Van Loan smiles grimly at the tableau being played out before him and sighs almost sadly. It looks like the Phantom will not be needed tonight to stem the fruits of crime after all. However, rather than take his leave immediately, the masked crime fighter remains hidden in his place of darkness to view the thief's capture. After all, the cop is still alone and he might run into trouble. Van Loan knows that the officer might need help if the thief resists arrest, or is armed, so the Phantom Detective will remain vigilant, ready to act if needed.

The Phantom reluctantly holsters his snub-nose .38, as he notes that the big red-headed cop now has his own .38 Police Special drawn and ready for action, for the cop has now noticed the descending thief.

Richard Curtis Van Loan smiles grimly, knowing that the thief will soon get the surprise of his life and his just desserts.

Downward, step by step, carefully, slowly, the thief moves lower upon the fire escape ladder as the patient lawman awaits him with gun drawn ready to make his arrest.

Van Loan's eyes peer through the slits of the black silk mask stretched across his face with intense interest and a bit of amusement at the fate of this wily criminal robber. He watches the cop now waiting underneath the ladder in the darkness of the alley where the thief can not see him, waiting patiently for the thief to drop down to the ground and fall right into his arms to be arrested.

Slowly the ladder descends carrying the thief and finally the criminal with his bag of swag, alights upon the wet, cold cobblestones of the alley. No sooner does the man hit the ground than the policeman moves into view, gun drawn meaningfully.

The robber now gets a good look at the cop but he is not startled, nor does he resist or flee. The Phantom looks upon the scene with renewed interest; something does not seem right here. He rivets his attention on the thief and the cop in an effort to view all that is transpiring between them, being careful not to miss a single word spoken by the two men.

"Had a good night of it, did you, Ernie?" the cop finally asks the robber he has just caught red-handed, but in an unusual conversational manner. He has not arrested the thief as yet, nor subdued him or placed him in handcuffs. Van Loan is surprised the two men not only know each other, but they know each others names.

"I did all right, Tommy. I think he'll be pleased, which is all I care about now," Ernie Bilk replies to the cop. The thief does not seem concerned that a cop is there waiting for him, nor that he has been apparently caught red-handed after a robbery with the evidence in his possession.

What is going on here, Van Loan thinks.

"That's all you should ever care about, doing what he tells you," the cop replies in a tough tone.

The masked man watching and hearing it all from his place of concealment grows alarmed. These two men, one an upholder of the law and the other a thief engaged in a criminal act, know each other a bit too well. Then he is astounded when the cop holsters his gun and moves closer to the thief as if the two men are friends or working together. Soon the thief hands over a small sack to the cop. That can only be the swag from his robbery.

"Here it is. Give it to him. Tell him I did what he told me to do. Tell him… I don't want to do this no more. I don't want no trouble. You know him, he may be the Devil but I'll not do his bidding ever again. I'm finished with him now," the thief stammered, looking around him nervous, fearful, but serious.

"He'll not be happy to hear that when I tell him, Ernie," the cop replies coldly. "Why be so hasty? You know what I'm saying?"

"It's my decision, I did all that was asked of me, now I'm done."

"Yes you are," The policeman nods slowly, almost sadly, looking at the bag of stolen jewelry, hefting it in his hand he smiles. He opens the bag and looks inside to inspect the goodies. It is a fortune in gold and jewels. "Nice load. I know he will be pleased with this. You won't have to worry no more, you paid your debt."

"Paid in full now, right, Tommy?"

"That's right," Tommy laughs as a cold dark tone has crept into his voice that has just a hint of terrible menace. "Have no fear, the Devil will never darken your door again."

Ernie sighs in relief, "That's all I want. I'll never talk, my lips are sealed. Just tell him I'm done, then he can leave me be once and for all."

"Once and for all. I'll tell him. But there's just one little problem remaining that we need to clear up."

"Wha -- What problem?" the thief stutters fearfully.

"It's just this, Ernie; now that you're free of him like you always wanted, he's free of you too. You see, now The Devil has no further use for you…"

"So? What do you mean?"

"You know how it is," Then the policeman drew his handgun and the alley trembled with the thunder of a loud report. One slug entered Ernie's chest at close range and he fell to the ground motionless. He never made a sound.

Richard Curtis Van Loan is astounded by what he has just heard and witnessed. It was nothing less than the cold-blooded murder of a criminal by a city policeman; a policeman who should have simply arrested that criminal. Instead the lawman executed him. Van Loan is momentarily reeling, he's not seen this kind of wanton violence and brutality since his days in the Great War. He's witnessed a terrible bloody scene, but one that has left him with more questions than it has given him answers. He knew that what he'd just seen wasn't as simple as it looked, for both men's words held severe implications for the city he loved, for the Police Department he respected, and for The Phantom himself. And just who was this man they called Devil? Did he, in fact, really exist?

Van Loan watched as the policeman made sure that Ernie Bilk was indeed dead. Then, hefting the little bag of jewels victoriously, the cop holstered his gun and began to walk to the alley opening that led to the street beyond. He would be gone in a minute if he was not stopped.

Van Loan was aghast by what he had seen. He could not allow a city policeman to get away with murder but he also knew there was more behind this than the simple greed and corruption of a single cop. Nor even the cold-blooded murder of a lowly thief. He had heard both men mention a third man they apparently worked for. That man they both referred to as the Devil. The thief had been terrified of him. The crooked cop was clearly working for him. Both men were obviously this Devil's minions and Van Loan knew he had to discover the identity of the man who pulled the strings on the crime and murder he had witnessed here tonight in this dark alley behind The Ascot Hotel. Idly he wondered how many more crimes this man was involved in. What Van Loan had seen and heard tonight surely must be just the tip of the iceberg. There might be a vast unknown criminal network here that needed looking into and he realized the danger instantly. Here was an unknown and unsuspected super criminal organizing crime in his city with impunity. He was doing his evil work hidden from everyone's eyes and getting away with it. Or worse, and this really put fear into Van Loan, it was obvious this Devil was some kind of super criminal who had serious and deep connections with powerful people in his city who protected him. He must be stopped at all costs and the first step in accomplishing that was taking down this crooked cop.

With utter silence and great speed the ace crime fighter made his way through the inky blackness of the alley towards the unsuspecting policeman. The Phantom came upon the man from behind, grabbing the cop with a tight arm across his throat as his snub nose .38 pressed meaningfully into the temple of the surprised man. The cop immediately understood what was happening and his body went limp, too scared to fight back. Then The Phantom dragged the policeman backwards into the depths of darkness deep inside the alleyway.

"Don't make a sound," the Phantom warned in a gritty whisper full of anger, his lips an inch away from the cop's ear. The cop was now frozen in fear. He was sweating profusely. The Phantom quickly withdrew the cop's gun and threw it to the ground while he rapidly dragged the man backwards still deeper into the inky darkness of the alley where he would soon begin his grim work to extract answers to his questions. The Phantom would make this cop talk. He would make this crooked cop spew all he knew about the robbery, of course, but what he really wanted to know was everything about the man behind all this handiwork, the master criminal who pulled the strings, the man they had called the Devil.

"I did as you told me," the cop blubbered softly, clearly terrified now by the mysterious powerful figure who had surprised him so thoroughly and held him helpless.

"As I told you?" The Phantom whispered the question, not quite understanding what the man meant at first. Then it dawned on him that the cop may have mistaken him for someone else. Perhaps the cop had mistaken him for this mysterious Devil? If so, then it appeared the man did exist. This knowledge only spurned The Phantom to grow more determined to get to the bottom of this grotesque mystery.

"Did I tell you to kill that man?" The Phantom asked in whispered response.

Now, Tommy the cop, began to shake with utter terror. He cried out in a low mewling voice, "No! No, I made the decision myself when I heard what Ernie told me. I knew he would be of no further use to you. I know how you don't like to keep useless people around. You don't like to leave loose ends."

"Noooo…but you presumed…" the Phantom growled, trying to play the part of the man the crooked cop thought he was.

"I'm sorry! Don't kill me! I've always been loyal. I would never betray you!" the cop stammered. The Phantom was amazed at the hold this Devil character had on such a tough copper. The cop couldn't see the man who held him helplessly from behind and Van Loan made sure to keep it that way. The cop had no idea the Phantom Detective held him captive.

"Tell me everything I ask and I promise that it will go easier for you," the Phantom warned in a gruff tone.

The cop suddenly stopped shaking, and Van Loan could tell the man was thinking it through, then he sighed in evident relief and a hint of boldness crept into his manner as he realized the truth," You're…you're not *him*!"

"But I work for *him*," the Phantom responded immediately, hoping he had not given the game away and could recoup his advantage over his captive.

The cop remained silent for a moment then a smile crossed his face, "No. No you don't work for him, or I would already be dead. You're not *him* and you don't work for *him*!"

"You're right, but I'm worse than *him*. I'm the Phantom!" Van Loan growled in a low bestial rage. "You've heard of me?"

"Y-Yes, of course, but please…" Tommy the cop trembled, for he had heard about the Phantom as had all inhabitants of the city and he was terrified of the man. The Phantom was rumored by some to be an ace crime fighter who took no prisoners, or a super criminal who was a deadly killer, by others. It depended on who you heard the story from. Of course, The Phantom was neither, not exactly, but everyone feared him with good reason. In any case it meant double danger for anyone who ever crossed his path and the cop knew that, but there was someone he feared even more. "He'll kill me. I can't talk."

"I'll kill you if you don't talk!" The Phantom warned in a deadly voice, and meant it.

Tommy the cop swallowed nervously, gasping for breath as the Phantom still held him tightly by the throat. "You don't understand. He has powers. He knows things no one else knows. He see things other men do not. Oh my God, he is probably watching us right now!"

"That's ridiculous!" The Phantom laughed grimly at the man's paranoia, in an effort to stem the fear of his captive and get him to talk. "No one will ever know what you tell me."

Suddenly the second loud report of the evening broke the quiet of the night to echo in the darkness of the alley. Tommy the cop's head soon grew wet and sticky with running blood.

The Phantom held the wounded man in his arms, but his eyes frantically scanned the area in the direction the shot had come from, but he could see nothing in the pitch blackness. His keen hearing listened for movement, running feet, anything to tell him where the assassin was, but he heard nothing. Van Loan slowly and carefully placed Tommy the cop down to the cold cobblestones, resting his head on a pile of old *Clarion* newspapers. He could see that the life was draining out of the cop and that the man would soon be dead. No ambulance or doctor could help him now. Van Loan was running out of time to get the answers he needed.

The Phantom looked into Tommy's face, deep into his eyes, as the blood drained out of him. The man had scant minutes to live. "Tell me! Who is this Devil? Give me a name! Tell me now!"

"I-I…c-can't…" Tommy coughed blood, starring up in terror into the face of The Phantom Detective. That face was covered by a black silk mask with just two slits cut into it where the man could see his blazing eyes. "You have eyes like him, you know? I knew he would find me after you caught me. Pray you never meet him. I am but one of his minions, but there are many more like me. He is the Devil and he is all powerful."

"Tell me! Who is this Devil?"

"Tell me about him!" Van Loan barked in anger. "Give me a name!"

"There is nothing to tell. You will never find him, but he will find you when the time is right," the cop sputtered weakly, then he closed his eyes and died.

• • •

"Go right in, Mr. Van Loan. Mr. Havens is expecting you," the attractive brunette told the good-looking young man who had just entered *The Clarion* newspaper offices. Richard Curtis Van Loan had not seen this particular young woman before, but she reminded him of his secret love; Havens' own daughter, Muriel. This new girl must have been recently added to *The Clarion* payroll by publisher Frank Havens. Van Loan flashed her a warm smile as he quickly walked into the office of her boss.

Once Van Loan had entered Havens office and closed the publisher's door securely behind him, the attractive young secretary picked up her telephone and quickly dialed a special number, speaking softly into the mouthpiece.

• • •

"Van, good to see you," Frank Havens said with cordial friendship, using the short version of the playboy's name. "Come on in, take a seat. We have a lot to discuss."

"Yes we do," Van Loan stated to the older man in a firm tone obviously upset by what had transpired the night before.

"Well, before you ask, let me tell you the case is closed. The cops are happy, they have their fallen hero. The citizens of the city can sleep peacefully at night and you don't have to scare them with talk of some criminal organization that does not exist."

Van Loan was astounded and stood silently for a long moment. He could not believe what he had just heard. The publisher of the city's biggest and most influential newspaper, and his best friend, seemed to be participating in some kind of cover-up! Not only covering up two murders, but denying the very existence of the man who was behind it all. Van Loan was outranged and was about to tell Havens his thoughts on the matter when the man immediately commanded his attention.

The newspaper magnate suddenly put his finger to his lips indicating their conversation should immediately cease. Havens quickly pointed to the small wooden box on his desk; his office intercom. He said not a word, but pointed out to Van Loan that the red light had now suddenly gone on. Van Loan was surprised but he knew what that meant. It indicated their conversation was now being listened to by Havens' new secretary in the outer office. She was either a very nosy young lady or she herself was a minion! He wasn't sure how much of their conversation she had heard, but it appeared she had just opened the line to listen in. If that was the case, perhaps not all was lost. Perhaps it could even be used to their advantage.

Havens said not a word, but now quickly scribbled a note and showed it to his friend.

FOLLOW MY LEAD NOW
I WILL EXPLAIN ALL LATER

Van Loan looked at his friend with surprise but nodded, deciding to play along for now.

"So, Van," Havens began once again, motioning with his hand for his friend to follow his lead for the benefit of their listener, "To sum it all up, I think it looks like the cops are correct on what happened. A rather simple crime. Poor Officer Prentiss was a hero, killed by the robber's partner, yet to be found. He will probably never be found. The police have no leads. It's a terrible tragedy. Case closed."

"Yes..." Van Loan replied softly, forcing himself to sound convincing, "I read about it this morning in your paper of course, and I believe you're correct. It makes sense. A common robbery gone bad."

"*The Clarion* has reported the story this morning just as the police have given it to me."

"Good, then that is all settled and there is nothing else for us to discuss now," Van Loan stated, hoping that would sate the curiosity of their eavesdropper.

"Yes, that settles it. Thanks for dropping by and saying hello. You know, you must come by the house some day, spend some time."

"I will, Frank. I will. Well, for now I guess I'd better be off, so I'll say my goodbye and be on my way," Van Loan said briskly, all for the benefit of their listener in order to allow her time to appear that she was back and busy at work.

Frank Havens smiled and let out a deep breath as he pointed to the intercom on his desk. The red light had just gone off. Their listener was no longer listening.

"See you later," Havens whispered to his friend.

Richard Curtis Van Loan nodded and shook hands with Frank Havens and then left his friend's office. On the way out he carefully noted the pretty young secretary in Frank's outer office, and casually said goodbye to her. He was shocked that this Devil may have gotten a spy into Frank Havens office!

• • •

Later that night at the posh estate of Richard Curtis Van Loan a car pulled up the drive and Frank Havens got out and entered the massive house. He was alone.

"Good to see you, Frank," Van Loan said as he ushered his friend into his private library. He made a drink for himself and Havens as the two men sat down to talk. "I gave the servants the night off tonight. We're alone now. We need to talk."

"Just the two of us then," Havens stated with a smile. "I imagine you have a lot of questions."

"I'll say. The Phantom made a visit to that alley in the back of the Ascot Hotel last night," Van Loan stated in a sharp tone. "I want some answers, Frank."

Havens nodded grimly, he was the all powerful editor and publisher of the city's leading newspaper, *The Clarion*. He was also Van Loan's best friend and the only man who knew his secret; that the young man who acted the pampered playboy Richard Curtis Van Loan was actually the notorious Phantom Detective. Havens and Van Loan worked together, the newspaper magnet being the man who set the Phantom Detective upon his cases. It had been that way for years now, since the younger man had returned from the Great War. He still craved the excitement he had grown used to on the battlefield and realized that he could not live without it. Now he fought crime as a masked avenger in a relentless war upon the battlefield that was New York City and it had become his prime mission in life.

"I heard about it all from the police. Inspector Armitage called me earlier and gave me all the details," Havens said matter-of-factly.

"Really? Well, it is an interesting case. I just wish you would have waited for my report before going to press. I would never believe what happened if I had not been there and seen it all with my own eyes, heard their words with my own ears," Van Loan stated.

"Yes, it must be a lot to take in at once: a fantastic robbery, two murders, a dead cop who could have been a valuable witness," Havens replied thoughtfully.

"The cop's murder stymied my investigation last night, but it's not just the two murders, it's the other thing that has me intrigued. This man they called the Devil. He seems to have a fairly large organization, and a very professional one. He also seems to instill utter fear into his minions. Much like the real Devil would. They both spoke of him, mentioned him by that name, so he must exist, Frank."

"Come on now, don't tell me you believe this supernatural mumbo jumbo?" Havens asked with a laugh.

"Not supernatural, Frank, super criminal! We have a problem in this city that we had no idea ever existed. That cop, Tommy Prentiss, was murdered so he wouldn't talk. He was killed right in front of me. It was all done very neat and quick, by a real pro, who only took one shot. A sniper assassin. I was waiting for a second shot for me. It never came. Had he tried a second shot to take me down, I would have gotten his location tracked him down, but he knew his job too well. He only did what was necessary. This Devil himself, or most probably another of his minions, as they seem to call themselves, was in that alley last night. Watching, waiting, ready to act should he need to do so, and he did. He murdered Tommy Prentiss before I could get anything out of him. He was obviously posted there for that very reason, and that denotes careful planning of a special nature. This man needs to be brought down!"

"Look, Van, you did a great job last night, but we are sticking to the story. I got wind of this Ernie Bilk, a career thief and middling second-story man, when I heard he was casing the Ascot. So I gave you the lead. You stopped the robber from getting away. The stolen jewels were recovered and returned to the Ascot Hotel and are now back in the safe. In the commotion, the thief was shot dead by the cop; no doubt he was resisting arrest and deserved it. And the cop? Well, he was shot by one of the thief's confederates. The thief had a partner, one the cops have not found yet. That's what the cops told me, and that's what I printed this morning in *The Clarion*. That cop, Tommy Prentiss, is a hero, and he'll be buried as a hero," Havens stated thoughtfully, carefully looking at his best friend and seeing how upset he was by his words. Frank Havens knew following this case further at this point could only get his young friend killed. Then he said forcefully, "That's the way it must go down for now."

Van Loan shook his head, "I won't accept that. The Phantom will not accept that."

Havens stated grimly, "Look, Van, you see what we're up against now? That young lady *in my own office!* I'm not sure if she's on the Devil's payroll or just nosy, but we can't afford to take any chances until we know what we are dealing with."

"I understand, Frank. I was thinking about that too. This Devil is a lot more dangerous than I ever suspected. If he was able to get one of his minions into your office, then I fear that even the Police Commissioner or even the Mayor could be compromised. Nevertheless, I will not accept the cover up of two murders, nor the denial of his existence," Van Loan replied firmly, then adding, "And that's why I'm going to begin this case right now. With your new secretary, who by the way is the only lead we have, being the only living witness."

"Well, I rather doubt you will ever find her, Van. She told me she had a family emergency and left my office shortly after you did. She said she would not be back." Havens stated sadly, adding, "If she is one of this Devil's minions, she is no doubt missing, most likely already dead. You'll never find her."

Van Loan sighed and nodded gravely, then said firmly, "I'm sure she's missing but she's certainly not dead."

"How do you know she's not dead?" Havens asked curtly.

"Because I have her here, upstairs."

Havens looked curiously at his young friend for some kind of explanation.

"Look, Frank, he was able to get someone into your office, you're in danger too. It's time to get to work on this case. I'm going to start with her now and get some answers." Van Loan said forcefully. "Do you want to join me?"

To say that Frank Havens is surprised by this turn of events is certainly an understatement, but he recovers quickly and slowly nods his ascent.

"Good," Van Loan replies boldly. "To conceal my identity I'll change into my Phantom clothing and mask. I have her cuffed in a chair upstairs, secure and facing a long and empty wall. When you enter the room just stand by the door and she will not be able to see you. She'll only see me and I'll do all the talking."

The two men went up to the secret room. Van Loan was now dressed in the dark garb of the Phantom and entered the room to behold a sight that caused his blood to freeze.

"Quick, Frank, get the medical kit in the bathroom! She's slit her wrists. She may already be dead, poor girl."

Van Loan ran over to the pretty brunette in an effort to stop her bleeding but it was hopeless. She had used a hidden file to slit her wrists and the floor was covered in two large pools of blood. Her head was down, her body limp, her skin pale. She'd lost too much blood.

Richard Curtis Van Loan realized now that he'd never even known the young lady's name, in rage he shouted, "Why? *Why!*"

The young woman barely raised her head before she died to look sadly into his eyes and whisper, "The Devil made me do it, sir."

NOT THE END

The Phantom and Me

The Phantom Detective was one of the longest-running hero pulp characters who ever appeared during the classic era of the pulp magazines, from the 1930s on to the 1950s. It was an amazing run! The Phantom Detective pulp magazine was published for about 20 years, attesting to the rabid popularity of this fascinating hero. The Phantom, wealthy playboy Richard Curtis Van Loan, was the quintessential rich guy crime fighter and he was of the best. I love the original stories—writing by a host of authors back in the day—and it was a wonderful privilege for me to be allowed to write my own contribution to the series, "The Devil's Minions." In my story I bring to the Phantom canon one of his most dangerous and unusual cases that twists and turns like the coils of a great snake. I hope you enjoy reading this tale as much as I enjoyed writing it. Stay tuned for the next pulse-pounding novel in the sage of The Phantom vs The Devil!